gretta-

THE TUMBLING FIGURE WAS APPROACHING THE BOTTOM.

The X Bar X Boys on Big Bison Trail.   *Frontispiece (Page 170*

THE X BAR X BOYS ON BIG BISON TRAIL

BY

JAMES CODY FERRIS

AUTHOR OF "THE X BAR X BOYS ON THE RANCH,"
"THE X BAR X BOYS ON WHIRLPOOL RIVER," ETC.

ILLUSTRATED BY

WALTER S. ROGERS

NEW YORK
GROSSET & DUNLAP
PUBLISHERS

Made in the United States of America

WESTERN STORIES FOR BOYS

By JAMES CODY FERRIS

THE X BAR X BOYS BOOKS

THE X BAR X BOYS ON THE RANCH
THE X BAR X BOYS IN THUNDER CANYON
THE X BAR X BOYS ON WHIRLPOOL RIVER
THE X BAR X BOYS ON BIG BISON TRAIL
THE X BAR X BOYS AT THE ROUND-UP

(OTHER VOLUMES IN PREPARATION.)

GROSSET & DUNLAP, PUBLISHERS, NEW YORK

CONTENTS

CHAPTER		PAGE
I	THE CABIN	1
II	WHAT OF THE GORILLA?	11
III	THE HYPNOTIST	20
IV	BUG EYE'S CONTROL	28
V	A STARTLING CRY	38
VI	STARTING A CHASE	47
VII	THE HOLD-UP	55
VIII	MOVIE FOLK	64
IX	POP SCORES	73
X	NICK LOOKER II	82
XI	ADAM'S APPLE	92
XII	A TALE OF THE APE	102
XIII	THE LAWYER	109
XIV	OFF TO BISON TRAIL	117
XV	IN THE QUICKSAND	125
XVI	A LARIAT RESCUE	132
XVII	THE REARING BRONCO	141
XVIII	JUST IN TIME	153

CHAPTER		PAGE
XIX	OFF ON LOCATION	159
XX	DOWN THE MOUNTAIN	166
XXI	THE BIRTHMARK	174
XXII	PLANNING A SURPRISE	182
XXIII	A BLOT OF INK	190
XXIV	IN COURT	198
XXV	A JOVIAL JUDGE'S DECISION	205

THE X BAR X BOYS ON BIG BISON TRAIL

CHAPTER I

THE CABIN

DELICATELY, with almost the precision of an artist flecking the last spot of color on a completed picture, a gray mustang picked his way over a field dotted with gopher holes. His rider, a fair-haired boy of seventeen, whose blue eyes seemed to hold something of the freshness of the range in them, sat limp in the saddle, allowing the pony to make his own pace. The rains dangled loosely over the bronco's neck, and the hand that held them rested carelessly on the pommel.

The boy raised his head, and, squinting his eyes against the glare of the midday sun, peered ahead.

"Roy should be showing up pretty soon," he muttered. "Snakes, it's hot, and this is only May! Wait till July rolls around—we'll dry up and blow away then, I reckon." Bending over, he brushed a fly from the pony's

1

ear. "Shake 'em off, Flash! Those blue-bottles bite like sin."

A steep hill loomed ahead, and the boy clucked to his bronco.

"Take it on high, Flash, old boy. Maybe Roy is waiting for us at the top. He said San-born's Point, and here we are."

The horse quickened his pace obediently and galloped forward. As he and his rider breasted the rise a long "Y-o-o-o-o!" winged its way over the prairie. The rider answered, and stood still. In a moment another horse-man came into view.

"Yay, Teddy!" the new arrival called. "Get it?"

"Yep," Teddy answered. "Got it, Roy. And I had some ride back! Hotter than seven kinds of tarpots in those mountains. But here she is," and he motioned down toward a bundle that hung from the saddle horn.

A glance at these two boys would instantly flash a word into the observer's mind—broth-ers. True, one was light and the other dark—but each had the same facial characteristics, the same set of shoulders and head. Roy Man-ley, who had ridden in from the ranch to meet Teddy, was the elder by one year. He it was who inherited the dark hair and eyes from his father, owner of the X Bar X. Yet, strangely enough, he was more inclined to his mother's disposition—serious, grave, thoughtful. The

mother had been a teacher of English in a
school near Denver before her marriage, and
Roy took from her his love for books and poetry and, as Teddy remarked, "the blooming
sunsets." Roy was the family philosopher.

Teddy Manley, on the other hand, had the
hair and eyes of his mother and the happy,
carefree, joyful nature of his father. He could
never quite understand what Roy saw in the
contemplation of a mountain at night, or of a
river flashing beneath the morning sun.

"Golly," he would say, "you see that blamed
thing day after day, night after night, and still
you stand and moon at it! It'll be there to-
morrow! Come on, let's eat!"

Roy would smile and turn away. But a half
hour later might find him carefully balancing
a tricky can of water over the door, just as
Teddy was expected in. Roy was not *entirely*
taken up with the sunsets of life.

Teddy yawned, and closed his teeth with an
unexpected snap as Flash, his bronco, twitched
suddenly to dislodge a persistent fly.

"Yep, I had some hot ride," the boy repeated. "Started at six this morning. And I'm
just a *leetle* tired. Belle ought to be satisfied
with this," and again he gestured toward the
package hung on his saddle.

Belle was the sister of these boys. She
was thirteen that day, and Teddy had ridden
twenty miles to get her a present.

"Let's take a peek at it," Roy suggested eagerly. "Does it look real?"

"I'll say it does! Here—unwrap it, if you want to." He passed the bundle over to his brother.

Roy broke the cord and carefully unfolded the paper. As the wrapping came off, his horse gave a wild snort and reared.

"Jiminy, even Star thinks it's real!" Roy cried delightedly. "Here, Star—down! Snap out of it! Say, Teddy, isn't it a beauty?"

He held up the object. It was a "honey" bear—stuffed. The resemblance to life was perfect. The taxidermist who had prepared it had caught the true naturalness of the little animal, and, as Roy held it, the bear actually looked as though he were sniffing at one of Roy's hands. The taxidermist had been a real artist.

"It sure looks as if it was alive," Teddy chuckled. "See how the head is bent, as if he was smelling something good to eat! That boy in Los Dipono is sure a genius when it comes to stuffing Teddy Bears!"

"I'll tell a maverick he is!" Roy agreed. "When Belle sees this she'll go crazy. She always wanted a Teddy Bear, and when she knows you rode twenty miles to Dipono you'll be the white-haired boy around the ranch. How'd you hear of this fellow who stuffs animals, anyway, Teddy?" Roy asked, as he wrapped the bear up again.

"Nick Looker told me about him. Oh, by the way, I saw some one that I could have sworn was Nick just as I left Dipono. But Nick was at the ranch this morning, wasn't he?"

"Nope, he wasn't." The two boys clucked to their horses, and moved toward home. "He asked dad for leave last night to visit somebody—didn't say who—and he wasn't back when I left."

"Yea?" Teddy questioned and considered for a moment. "That's funny. Maybe it was Nick, then. But what would he be doing in Los Dipono? That's a joke town—three stores, a few houses, and the shack where the taxidermist lives that I bought the bear from. What would Nick be doing in such a place?"

"You got me." Roy shrugged his shoulders. "But I do know one thing—Nick has been pretty restless lately. He's expecting some money, you know."

"That's right—an inheritance. Hope he gets it. Nick is regular, if anyone ever was." Teddy glanced at the sky behind him, observed a hill of black clouds piling up, and touched his heels to Flash's sides. "Step on it, Roy; it's going to rain."

Roy nodded absently. "Your seeing Nick in Dipono interests me," he declared. "Do you think his going there could have anything to do with the money he's expecting?''

"I don't think anything," Teddy replied and grinned. "I'm too hot and tired. Later I'll give you my valuable opinion on the subject. Just now what interests me most is beating that storm home. Swing into it, Flash!"

The two boys galloped along the range. Teddy looked over at Roy, and laughed.

"Still worrying about Nick?" he asked. "You must have a one-track mind, Roy. In the first place, I'm not sure whether it was Nick or not. I saw him for only a minute. Anyway, we can find out as soon as we get home."

"I know we can," Roy remarked. "But I was just thinking. You know Nick and Jules Kolto are pretty good friends now, and have been all winter."

Teddy nodded. Roy was referring to a hand on the X Bar X Ranch who, the previous fall, had taken some four hundred dollars from Mr. Manley's desk while the owner of the ranch was away trying to round up some of his cattle that had strayed from home. Kolto, who was at first known as Joe Marino, or more familiarly "The Pup," had admitted his theft after some exciting episodes, and said he was once a bandit, but that he wanted to make good now, and declared he would work for Mr. Manley until every cent of the four hundred was paid back. He had been with the X Bar X all winter, and he and Nick Looker had become fast friends.

"What I mean is," Roy continued, "that Nick would like to get his inheritance so he could lend Kolto the four hundred, or whatever is still owing, so he could pay dad back. Anyway, that's my guess."

"And I'll bet it's a wild one," Teddy laughed. "You always make a novel out of a perfectly simple state of facts. Say, did you get that sentence? Must remember that—make a novel out of a perfectly simple state of facts. Good, hey?"

"Yea, good and rotten," Roy replied, and grinned. "But what's the matter with my theory? Logical, isn't it?"

"Oh, so-so," Teddy answered carelessly. "It might be true. But what of it? Snakes, you sure do let a thing stick in your mind! Get a wiggle on, Roy, or we'll get soaked for certain!" He pointed to the darkening clouds which were piling up back of them.

In another few moments the sun was blotted out and an ominous grayness fell over the land. Even Roy began to appreciate their position, and urged Star to his best speed.

"Anyway, I bet I'm right!" he yelled as he sped along. "Watch out for that bear, Teddy —don't let it bounce like that! You'll smash it!"

Teddy seized the bobbing bundle under his

arm and let Flash "spread himself," as he called it. The Manley boys had no wish to be caught in a storm on this flat plain.

Far ahead of them they could see the Rocky Run River and beyond this a high mountain called Bitter Cliff. Between these two lay the X Bar X Ranch. In the clear air it seemed only a few miles distant, but both Teddy and Roy knew that they had almost an hour's ride ahead of them. The storm was coming rapidly now, and rumbles of thunder could be faintly heard in the distance.

"We'll never make it!" Roy shouted. "Take it easy, Teddy! We haven't a chance. Your bronc must be pretty tired, too, after your long ride. No use to run him for nothing."

"What'll we do, then?" Teddy asked, pulling Flash down to a walk. "She's coming fast, Roy! I don't especially care to take a bath here. It's only Wednesday."

"We can head for those trees." Roy laughed and gestured to one side. "Maybe we'll find some sort of shelter in there. I know I saw an old prospector's cabin some place around here, but I don't remember just where."

"We'll try it, anyway," Teddy declared, and swung Flash to the left. "We'll be partly protected by the trees, at least."

Roy followed his brother, and they reached the edge of the little grove of quakermasts just as the first huge drops began to fall. A fitful wind sprang up, which increased to a gale within two minutes. Then a vivid flash ripped the black sky, and the roar of thunder that followed seemed to shake the earth. Next came the rain—a flood of water that rode downward and ahead on a fierce wind, beating against the backs of the two boys. The trees bent low before the fury of the blast.

"Look for that cabin!" Teddy shouted, pulling his sombrero low over his face. "We'll be drowned here!"

Suddenly Roy gave a yell.

"Here it is! I thought I was right! Dive into it, Teddy! I'll take Flash and Star around back! No use of both of us getting soaked through! You take the bear!"

With a gesture of assent, Teddy slid from his pony and with the bundle under his arm ran for the shack—a low, one-roomed building set between two quakermasts. Not a very habitable place, but it would be dry—if the roof didn't leak too much!

Teddy reached the door and flung it open, pulling hard against the force of the wind. Within was darkness, the one window being boarded up.

"Dreary sort of a shack," Teddy thought, and shivered slightly. "Wonder who built this? Some guy that's dead by now, probably. Well—"

He stepped forward. As he did so he heard

a queer, scraping sound in front of him, as though a man, with long fingernails, were scrambling over the floor on his hands and knees. Choking in his throat a cry of surprise, the boy jumped back, beyond the door.

Then a grotesque body leaped for the opening. Resembling a man, yet there was something strangely inhuman about it. The arms were too long, the neck too short, the body too hairy. For a moment Teddy stood in dumb astonishment, unable to credit his eyes. His heart beat wildly.   Then he saw the figure bounding away through the rain, with shoulders hunched, and knuckles touching the ground at every step.

Teddy staggered back, his breath coming in short gasps. The realization came suddenly.

"Jumping lizards!" the boy panted. "A monkey! An ape! Great snakes! It's a gorilla!"

CHAPTER II

What of the Gorilla?

TEDDY MANLEY'S mind hardly grasped the significance of the thing he had seen. An ape —here! In this shack! There was no doubt about it; he was still eyeing the clump of bushes wherein the animal had disappeared. But what did it all mean? How could—

A terrific clap of thunder interrupted the boy's musing, and, recovering himself, he stepped gingerly within the door. He had a vague terror that there might be another of the monsters hiding in the darkness of the hut, but he shook the fear off and entered. At the same instant Roy, who had been behind the cabin, ran around the corner and jumped for the door.

"Whew!" he gasped. "Some rain! I'm wet through! Got the horses fixed up underneath a kind of shed in the rear. Star was sort of scared. Teddy! What under the sun's the matter? Did you see a ghost?"

"Pretty near," and Teddy grinned weakly. "Strike a light, will you? My matches are soaked."

11

Roy quickly brought forth a waterproof box of matches, and ignited one. The yellow glow flickered eerily on the bare walls of the cabin, and told Teddy the one thing he most wanted to know. The place was empty.

He gazed about him, and unconsciously sighed with relief.

"No more," he murmured, and hunched his shoulders with a meaning gesture.

"No more what?" Roy asked, eyeing his brother in astonishment. As the match went out he stepped forward and grasped Teddy by the arm. "What's this all about, Teddy! You look as white as a sheet. Snap to it now! What happened?"

"Plenty," Teddy answered. "I saw a gorilla."

"What?"

The exclamation fairly burst from Roy's lips, and he started back. "Say that again, Teddy. I must have gotten you wrong."

"Oh, you heard me," Teddy remarked. "It's a fact. I did see a gorilla. He was in here when I opened the door, and he jumped out and ran away through the rain."

"He ran away through the rain," Roy repeated slowly. "Yes. That's right. That's what all gorillas do—they run away through the rain. Here! Sit on this bench, Teddy. There! Feel better now?"

"Oh, I'm not crazy!" Teddy exclaimed

hotly, leaping to his feet. "It's true, I tell you! Here! Look at me!" He turned swiftly toward the open door, so that the light fell full upon his face! "Do I look as if I had gone nuts? Wait—I'll show you."

Oblivious of the rain that was still coming down in torrents, he walked to the front of the cabin and, bending over, examined the ground. Then he motioned for Roy to come nearer.

"See those?" he demanded, pointing to the earth. "What do you think made them?"

Roy, his eyes almost starting from his head, saw the imprints of two, huge animal-like hands sprawled in the mushy sod. Near them were four marks, close together, as though some giant had pressed his big knuckles to the ground.

"Jumping catamounts!" Roy gasped. "You're right, Teddy! These were made by an ape—and a big brute at that!"

"A gorilla," Teddy asserted positively. "A gorilla as tall, or almost as tall, as a man. I saw him as plainly as I see you now—saw him swing along and disappear in those bushes over there."

"Well, I don't know about the gorilla part," Roy said doubtfully. "I believe there's only one of those in captivity, and he's in Germany. It isn't likely—"

"But this one wasn't in captivity!" Teddy insisted. "He was roaming around, as free as you please! Didn't have a chain on him or anything. I was rushing for this shack to get in before I got all wet, and the minute I pulled open the door I heard a scrunching, scratching sound. Naturally I dodged back and just then this gorilla made a leap for the door and loped away, as calm as anything."

"Well, it sure beats me!" Roy declared, shaking his head. "But let's go in. It's like standing in a river out here." He led the way into the cabin. Once there, he lit another match, with a little laugh which would have fooled no one, however, not even himself. "Might find a candle," he explained, and Teddy grinned.

"Or something," the younger lad added. "Oh, you believe it all right, Roy, my boy. It was a gorilla, as sure as you're a foot high! Though how he got here I can't imagine."

"He must have escaped from a circus," Roy suggested. "Let's see—is there a circus?"

"Not one within five hundred miles," Teddy stated definitely. "Of course it's barely possible that he *did* escape from one, and wandered all the way down here. But it would take time to do that, and those apes are valuable. It seems to me the circus people would have been on his track as soon as he got loose."

"Maybe they are. But that's the only explanation I can think of. Certainly the West is no place to breed gorillas."

Teddy removed his sodden sombrero and

flung it on an old chair standing in one corner. The idea of a gorilla loose in this vicinity was a novel one, and one not entirely without excitement. Teddy thought of the many adventures he and Roy had had in the past year. Horse-thieves, kidnappers, bandits—but never, until now, a gorilla!

As the boy stood in the center of that darkened cabin, with the rain beating a tattoo on the roof, he recalled the chase after the rustlers who had stolen Star and Flash, and of the strange man who had aided them in their pursuit. This is related in the first book of this series, entitled "The X Bar X Boys on the Ranch." Then, following quickly on the heels of these adventures, came more, when Teddy and Roy rescued their sister and two of her friends from the hands of kidnappers, who had stolen the girls out of revenge for a fancied wrong done them by Mr. Manley, Roy and Teddy's father. The book concerned with this rescue is called "The X Bar X Boys in Thunder Canyon."

Later the two brothers were forced to take a perilous trip down Whirlpool River, to help their father round up some cattle that had wandered from the home range to the fields of a faraway ranch. The wanderings of these cattle had hardly been an accident, for the men who were sent to guard them had failed in their job. Because these men had not taken greater care of their charges, Teddy and Roy Manley had undergone some of the most exciting and dangerous adventures they had ever experienced. The story of that eventful trip on the fierce waters is told in the book just preceding this, called: "The X Bar X Boys on Whirlpool River."

All these scenes were flashing through Teddy's mind like pictures on the silver sheet. He himself could not have said exactly what had awakened the memories. Perhaps it was because this cabin so much resembled another in which he and Roy had taken shelter from just such a storm as this. Therein they had come upon an injured man who later changed the course of several lives. Now, in this dreary place, they had found, not a man, but an ape!

"Chances are we'll never see him again," Teddy muttered. "Likely he was more scared than I was."

"Teddy, quit that mumbling and speak up!" Roy said, with a laugh. "Since when did you form the habit of talking to yourself?"

Gradually the boys' startled senses were returning to normalcy, and they were able to view the occurrence from a more dispassionate angle. Teddy, knowing that Roy's laugh was an indication that he considered the danger, if any had really existed, to be over, grinned slightly.

"I was thinking that we've never had very

much experience with gorillas," he remarked, "and I'd hardly know how to treat one. Now suppose, Roy—," and a mischievous look came into Teddy's eyes—"suppose, Roy, you and I were standing here talking, as we're doing now, just about anything, and all of a sudden—"

Crash!

The storm, marching its sullen way to the east, had flung a last violent threat toward the earth. The bolt struck within a hundred feet of the cabin, toppling a majestic quakermast and sending it crashing down almost on the very roof.

Teddy, his words frozen on his lips, stood like a statue. Roy turned startled eyes toward the door.

"Suppose you confine your conversation to less exciting topics," Roy remarked, a trifle shakily. "If that had hit a bit nearer, we wouldn't be worrying about gorillas or anything else. Golly, that was quick! Guess it's the last, though. The rain's stopped."

He walked to the door and peered out. Far to the east could be seen the retreat of the aerial army, their black, mountainous troops flashing the thunderbolts at irregular intervals. The mutterings of their cannons were faintly heard. The storm was over.

"Well, do we sleep here or do we go home?" Teddy asked, as he watched his brother staring at the noble spectacle of the rolling rainclouds.

"What?" Roy turned suddenly, almost as though he were accosted by a stranger. Then he laughed. "Oh, sure, we'll go home. But isn't that great, Teddy—those black castles in the sky?"

"Huh? Black castles? Oh, you mean the storm! Yea, fine—only it's pretty wet. Come on, you mooner! Time we started! Don't suppose it would do much good to have a look for our friend?"

"The ape? Not any! Unless you have some salt you want to put on his tail, so you can bring him home for a pet. And gorillas have no tails, though they should have. Nope, we'll do with the bear you brought. And that reminds me"—both boys were now walking toward the rear of the hut, where the horses had been tied—"about Nick Looker. Do you think the money he is expecting had anything to do with his trip to Dipono?"

"Do you think the gorilla escaped from a circus or was he born here?" Teddy countered. "You answer my question and I'll answer yours. In the first place, as I said before, I'm not sure it was Nick." The boy approached his mount and affectionately patted the horse's side. "Well, Flash, how'd you like the rain? Nice and cool now?" He vaulted into the saddle, still holding to the package he had ridden so far to get, and Roy followed his example. As the two brothers rode out from the trees, Teddy turned and looked behind him.

"Call him," Roy grinned. "Say: 'Here, nice gorilla!' Too bad you haven't got some candy to offer him."

"That's all right—if you had seen him you wouldn't kid about it," Teddy snorted. "Baby, he was some mean-looking brute!"

"Yes, now that you mention it, I imagine he was," Roy answered quietly. " 'Scuse, Teddy. No more kidding. Your face was as white at though you'd seen a ghost when I walked into that hut. Lucky for you the beast didn't feel nasty. Say, I just thought of something! Are you going to tell about this at the ranch?"

"Why not?"

"Well," Roy said slowly, "it's sort of hard to credit. Of course dad will believe us, and mother. But what will the boys say? What will Pop say? A gorilla! And how many times have we kidded Pop for telling stories not half so improbable!"

"Hum! Never thought of that!" Teddy mused. "But they'll know some time—might as well have it over with. Believe it or not— it was a gorilla!"

Holding the package tightly under his arm, Teddy urged Flash into a gallop.

CHAPTER III

The Hypnotist

THE story of their adventure with the ape was delayed in its telling, for when the two boys reached home, tired and hungry, they found a pleasant surprise in the persons of Nell Willis and Ethel Carew, two friends of their sister's, who were staying with their aunt, Mrs. Ball, over at the 8 X 8 Ranch. Nell and Ethel, or more familiarly "Curly," had come from the East nearly a year ago, intending to stay but a few months. But business necessitated the going of their families to Europe, and Mr. and Mrs. Ball were most happy to entertain the two girls until their parents returned. The Easteners were rapidly becoming "Westernized," and their frequent visits to the X Bar X were far from displeasing to Teddy and Roy.

In celebration of Belle's birthday, Mrs. Manley had prepared a large dinner. The feature of the occasion was the presentation of the "Teddy Bear."

When Belle saw it emerge from its wrappings, she fairly shrieked with delight. Thir-

teen is not the age when girls find it difficult
to express their emotion.

"Teddy!" she screamed, and ran to her
brother. "I've always wanted one of those!
Isn't it—isn't it real looking!"

"Sure," Teddy grinned. "It's meant to be.
Scared Flash with it when I opened it to show
it to Roy."

"Honestly, Teddy, I do think it's sweet!" and
Belle gravely offered her brother a kiss. "So
that's why you left so early last night. *Where-
ever* did you get it?"

"Los Dipono," Teddy answered. "Nick
Looker told me about an old man there who is
a wonder at stuffing animals, and I thought I'd
give him a try."

Nell and Ethel had left their seats and were
crowded around Belle to observe the birthday
present.

"See how the head is bent!" Ethel exclaimed. "You almost expect it to roll over
and do a somersault or stand on its front legs.
They're the cutest things, Belle! I saw two of
them, alive in New York, with a circus. They
could box just like human beings."

"The word circus reminds me," Roy broke
in, turning to his father, who, concluding his
dinner, had drawn a corncob pipe from his
pocket and was filling it. Mr. Manley was a
large man, whose appearance was like that of
a grave, old-time, southern gentleman. This

effect was aided by a long, drooping mustache, with ends that curled nearly below his chin. But when one expected a solemn handshake and booming "how-do-you-do," one saw the twinkling eyes and was not at all surprised to receive instead, a clap on the back and a jolly: "Hi ya, friend! Put 'er there!" Bardwell Manley was a Westerner, pure and simple—though some of acquaintances would have argued the fitness of that last word.

At his son's remark he raised a protesting hand.

"Now, Roy," he laughed, "no circuses. You're a bit old for that sort of thing. Anyway, you'd sure get sick on popcorn."

"No, seriously, Dad, I want to know.   Is there a circus around here?"

"Not that I know of," Mr. Manley answered, drawing deep on the corncob. "Why, for Pete's sake?"

"Because—" Roy hesitated. "You tell him, Teddy. You saw it."

"Saw what?" Mrs. Manley interrupted. "What's all the mystery about, boys?"

"Well, I saw a gorilla!" Teddy burst out defiantly. "A live one, too!"

The sentence, uttered earnestly, caused those at the table to start in surprise. They demanded details, and Teddy, nothing loath, told of his experience in the hut. At first Mr. Manley and the others were inclined to treat it as a joke, but Teddy's face, as he continued with the story, plainly showed he was sincere.

"Now, that sure takes the cake!" Mr. Manley ejaculated. "I thought we had about everything else out here, but I never expected to hear of a gorilla. Sure you didn't imagine it, Teddy?"

"No, he didn't, Dad! Because I saw the tracks," Roy insisted. "It was a big ape of some kind. That's the reason I wanted to know about the circus. I thought it might have escaped."

"No circus within miles that I know of," came from his father. "How big was it?"

"Seemed like an elephant to me," and Teddy laughed a bit nervously. "If there had been a window handy I would have gone through it head first. The brute walked out the door like an old woman going to a tea, and wandered off. Sure was funny!"

"Teddy, you must have been terribly frightened," Nell impulsively exclaimed. "A horrible thing like that in the same room with you! Ugh!"

"Wasn't any too pleasant," Teddy agreed. "Shook me up some. But let's forget it. Got any more of that cake, Mom?"

Later that evening the boys wandered out to the bunkhouse. Both were anxious to find out if Nick Looker had actually been in Dipono, and wanted to ask him about further developments of his inheritance. They found him leaning against the side of the house, repairing a saddle. He glanced up as they approached, and Roy thought lines of worry seemed to crease the cowboy's forehead. But the dusk was closing in rapidly, and the light was poor, so it may have been a shadow. Certainly Nick's voice seemed cheerful enough.

"Howdy!" he called. "Have a seat." He grinned and motioned to the ground. Teddy and Roy threw themselves down beside him. "I been tryin' to mend this here saddle of mine. Almost decided to throw up the job an' get a new one. But I hate to do it—this here hunk o' leather fits me like an old glove."

"A saddle is like a hat—you hate to change," Teddy commented. "Say, Nick, where you been all day?"

"Who, me?" Nick looked up quickly, then down again. "Why, I just got in, Teddy. I asked yore dad for time off, an' he gave it to me. I had an errand to do."

"I see," Roy nodded. He knew it would not be polite to press the puncher further. In the West a man's business is strictly his own. "We were wondering, that's all. Anything new?"

"Bug Eye's here," Nick laconically returned. "He drove Miss Carew an' Miss Willis over. I expect you seen 'em already, hey?"

"Still raving over his Fishmobile?" Roy in-

quired, referring to a strange contraption Bug
Eye had made from an old flivver. Bug Eye was
a hand on the 8 X 8, Peter Ball's place.

"Naw, he's forgotten that long ago," Nick
replied. He got to his feet and slung the saddle over his shoulder. "Come in for a minute,
boys?" he questioningly invited. "Gettin'
pretty dark." He led the way into the lighted
bunkhouse. "Speakin' of Bug Eye, he's got a
new wrinkle. Hypnotism! Hearn tell of it?"

"Hypnotism!" both boys exclaimed almost
in the same breath.

"What under the sun does Bug Eye know
of hypnotism?" Teddy demanded.

"Nothin', but he thinks he does," and Nick
laughed. "He's out experimentin' on Pop now.
Says it works best when the moon's full, an'
there's a full moon to-night. Ought to be up
soon."

"But where is he?" Roy inquired delightedly. "I want to see this! Is he going to try
to hypnotize Pop?"

"Yep," Nick grinned. "To-night. He thrun
over his book on English—*threw*, I mean; he's
got me goin' now—an' he's devotin' himself
exclusively to the sci-ence of hyp-no-tism!"

"Jumpin' lizards, what next?" Teddy
groaned. "That Bug Eye is sure a whizz!
Hypnotism! When does it take place, Nick?
Soon?"

"Soon as the moon comes up. If you boys

want to see some fun, hang around. But don't tell no one else, or Bug Eye might balk. I got an' idea Pop is kiddin' him some."

"I wouldn't doubt it," Roy chuckled. "Where is he going to do it?"

"Outside here. Listen—here he comes now. Don't let on I told you. Make believe you don't know nothin' about it."

As Teddy and Roy heard a footstep outside, they turned their backs to the door, then, as Bug Eye entered, they looked about carelessly.

"Howdy, gents!" was Bug Eye's greeting. "Glad to see you. I am once more amongst those present. Can't seem to stay away from this place. Step in here, Pop," and the puncher moved aside.

Pop Burns, his face drawn into a mournful expression that was whimsical in the extreme, entered the shack. Pop was the oldest hand on the X Bar X, and baldheaded. At the sight of his face Teddy almost burst into laughter, but restrained himself in time, though with a hard effort.

"Pop an' me have been studyin'," Bug Eye said gravely. "Ain't we, Pop?"

Pop nodded solemnly.

"We have, Bug Eye. Studyin' deep an' dark secrets."

"See what I got here?" Bug Eye exclaimed proudly, and he held a book up. "Look at her! Read, an' grow wise!"

On the cover of the book, in gilt letters, were the words: "Hypnotism. Its Use and Abuse."

"It's a great thing," Bug Eye continued enthusiastically. "Cures you of anything! Pop an' I are goin' to give a demonstration soon as the moon comes up. An' here she comes, too!" He pointed out of the door. A golden moon could be seen peeping above the horizon. "Get the boys together, Nick—I want every one to see this. Pop makes an ideal subject. His brain is very—now—receptive."

"I guess I got a weak mind," Pop said in a slow, mournful tone. "A weak mind. Get the boys together, Nick. All right, Bug Eye."

There was no need to call the boys. They had evidently been waiting. Now they crowded into the bunkhouse. Bug Eye motioned to Pop to stand just outside the door.

"The exhibition is about to begin," he said pompously. "Yore attention, gents!"

CHAPTER IV

Bug Eye's Control

Placing Pop so that the moon shone full on his face, Bug Eye started to wave his hands about in a mysterious manner. Accompanying these wavings came in a low mutter:

"You are goin' to sleep—to sleep—just think of sleep—yore eyes are closin'—you feel tired—"

"I'll bet he does," came in a low voice from one of the audience. "Throw yore hair back out o' your eyes, Pop." A titter went the round of the assemblage. Pop was as bald as an egg.

"You waddies keep quiet!" Bug Eye exclaimed fiercely, turning around. "How can I hypnotize anyone with you jabberin' away?"

"All right—pipe down, boys," Gus Tripp said gravely. "Go ahead, Bug Eye. We won't disturb you none."

While this was going on, Pop stood as still as a statue, his eyes fixed in an uncanny stare. Bug Eye returned to his labors.

"Now you're asleep," he proclaimed in a monotone. "Yore mind is under my control. Everything I tell you—that you must do. I—"

"Tell him to—" a voice started. But a sibilent "Pipe down!" cut it off short.

"You are under my control," Bug Eye continued solemnly. "Now—are you asleep?"

"I am!" Pop answered in a spectral tone. "Sound asleep!"

Bug Eye turned to the audience and spread his hands wide.

"You see?" he said proudly. "He's hypnotized! Now he'll do anything I tell him."

"Honest will he, Bug Eye?" Nat Raymond asked eagerly. "Anything at all? Listen! I got an idea! You tell him to—"

"Aw, Nat, you jump in the lake!" Gus snorted. "Since when was you appointed spokesman? Now you listen. Here's my idea. I say we—"

"Yea, *you* say, do you?" Jim Casey interrupted. "How do you get that away? I say we take a vote! Pop stands here, ready to do anything at all. What are we goin' to have him do? We'll never get another chance like this again, boys! Might as well make it good! Bug Eye, you be chairman. Call the meetin' to order."

"But listen!" Bug Eye pleaded, a look of distress on his face. "This here is a scientific demonstration! This ain't no—now, political rally, nor nothin'! What you goin' to hold a meetin' for?"

"Why, to find out what we want Pop to do!"

Jim Casey answered, in surprise. "What do you suppose? Here he is, the old geezer, just itchin' to be bossed. He'll do anything you tell him, you say. Well, we want to make it good! See?"

"Bug Eye doesn't know just what to do," Teddy chuckled delightedly, nudging Roy. "He didn't count on this. Something tells me this will be rare!"

Bug Eye was vainly attempting to explain.

"Listen, you birds!" he was pleading. "Listen, now! I put Pop under, an' I'm responsible for him. I can't do nothin' rash."

"That's all right," Gus said soothingly. We'll take all the responsibility, Bug Eye. You just do what we say. Now let's have the meetin'. I'll be the chairman, if Buy Eye won't. I'm open to suggestions."

"Let's have him think he's a girl goin' to a pink tea!"

"Naw, that ain't no good. Make him be a ballet dancer. I can just see the baldheaded old coot waltzin' around—"

"Aw, that's N. G.! Listen! I vote we—"

"Hey, for the love of Pete!" Bug Eye interrupted. "I can't be here all night! Pop's been standin' there for five minutes now, waitin' for you birds to make up yore minds!"

"Well, he don't care!" Nat Raymond declared. "He's asleep, ain't he? He don't know nothin' of what's goin' on. An' Pop loves to sleep. All right, Gus, go ahead with the meetin'. I got the floor. Mr. Chairman, I move we have Bug Eye tell Pop he's a opera singer.''

"Anyone second that?" Gus yelled.

"Sure!" Jim Casey responded. "I second it!"

"All in favor say Aye!"

"N-o-o-o-o!" came the answer. "We hearn him sing before! Want to make us all sick?"

"Say, Jules, suppose you make a suggestion," Gus said, nodding at the puncher who stood at the edge of the ring. "You ain't said a word yet. How about it?"

"Well," Jules replied hesitatingly, "I heard tell that a feller who was hypnotized would think he was anyone that the—now—oper-a-tor told him. Pop here always wanted to be a three-card monte man. Supposin' Bug Eye tells him he's the best three-card monte man in the world, an' that he can skin anybody out o' their money? Then we can give him the three cards an' bet with him. Maybe—well, Pop ain't so good at cards usually—so maybe we could have some fun. Then when we won his money we could wake him up, show him the cash we took, an' have the laugh on him. Bet it 'ud cure Pop of wantin' to be a gambler."

"Good idee!"

"That's the stuff! Pop'll be sore as a pup when he wakes up an' finds he's lost!"

"Me, I'm for that!"

"All right, boys, just as you say," Bug Eye agreed. "Some one get some cards an' a bench. Now watch."

He approached Pop, and once more began his strange gestures.

"Pop," he declared solemnly, "you are now a gambler, an' the best gambler in the world. You are the original three-card monte man. You can't lose. Around you is a crowd of tin-horn sports from the East. You take these cards—where's them cards—you take these cards, an' do yore stuff. Here's the table."

Some one had procured the cards and a stool from the bunkhouse. The moon made the scene almost as bright as day, and all the men, and Teddy and Roy, moved closer to see the performance.

Pop took the cards and looked at them for a moment. He seemed oblivious to those about him. Then he selected three cards—the ace of diamonds, of hearts and of spades. Lifting these in the air, he displayed them.

"Lay-dies an' gents," he proclaimed in the monotoned voice of a circus barker, "we have here three cards—the aces of hearts, diamonds an' spades."

"It's workin'!" Bug Eye whispered excitedly. "Told you I could do it! Look at Pop—look at him!"

There was no need for this suggestion. The eyes of every man there were fixed on Pop

with a fascinated stare. Teddy and Roy were
peering at him eagerly, waiting to see what
would happen next. Certainly the veteran
puncher corresponded with their ideas of what
a hypnotized man should look like. Pop's
face was alight with a new interest. Even his
voice seemed different. He gazed about him
brightly, as though he were, in truth trying
to entice a crowd of "sports" into a friendly
game.

"Either he's hypnotized or a mighty good
actor," Teddy whispered to his brother. "He
doesn't recognize one of us!"

"Watch," Roy cautioned in a low voice.
"He's going to do his stuff."

"Lay-dies an' gents!" Pop called once more.
"With these three cards I shall endeavor to
demonstrate a scientific fact—that the hand is
quicker than the eye."

"Where'd Pop learn all them big words?"
Gus whispered tensely.

"Don't know! Keep quiet! It's the hypnotism that's workin'!" Nat Raymond answered.

"Now, my friends," Pop went on, "I do not
desire to fool you in any shape, manner or
form. First I will show you how easy it is.
Now watch for the ace of spades."

He brought his hands together. The cards
crossed, then flew apart. "Who will tell me
where the ace of spades is?"

"Go ahead, Gus—show him," Jules whispered. "It's the end card."

"I think it's this one," Gus said slowly, pointing out the end card and gazing at Pop as though he expected the old man to shoot forth a tongue of fire from his mouth.

"Right you are!" Pop exclaimed loudly, disclosing the black ace. He looked at Gus as though the puncher was a stranger. "Try it again, mister?"

"Sure!" Gus replied, gaining courage now that nothing had happened.

Once more the cards came together and then separated.

"There she is!" Gus declared, and flipped over the card, the same ace of spades.

A frown apeared for a moment on Pop's face, but vanished as quickly.

"Yo're fast, mister," he said solemnly. "There's few men alive who can get the best of Frisco Lew twice, the way you done."

Bug Eye turned delightedly to Teddy. "He thinks he's Frisco Lew! Now we can get him! Say, Frisco," he went on pompously, swaggering forward, "I'd just like to make a little bet with you that I can tell you where that ace is every time."

Pop looked at Bug Eye casually and asked:
"You want to bet with Frisco Lew?"

"Yep!"

"I'm warnin' you—nobody ever won money

from me as long as I been a gambler! I'm the world's best three-card monte man!''

"That's all right," Bug Eye answered, winking at the others. "I don't mind losin' a little. Go ahead, shoot 'em out."

Carefully Pop arranged the cards. A tiny cloud drifted over the face of the moon, bringing darkness, but it passed in a moment and again the scene was brightly illuminated. Pop brought his hands together. The cards dropped to the bench.

"I'm bettin' one spondulix that this card is the ace of spades," Bug Eye declared, drawing a dollar from his pocket and laying it on a card.

Pop hesitated a moment, and appeared to be thinking. Then he reached into his own pocket and covered the bet.

"Turn 'er up," he said calmly, waving his hand.

Bug Eye obeyed—and disclosed the ace of spades.

"That's one you lose, Frisco," he snickered, picking up the money. "Try 'em again?"

Pop looked down at the cards as though he could not believe his eyes. Slowly he shook his head.

"Can't understand it," he muttered. "I never lost before. Well, this time I'll win! I'm the best gambler in the world—I can't lose!"

He took up the cards. This time he looked at Bug Eye keenly.

"I don't know yore name, mister," he declared, "but I want to tell you that yo're the one an' only man that ever beat Frisco Lew. I don't know where you come from, nor anything about you. But once more I'll try you."

He lowered his head. The cards flew apart.

"Now wait," Pop said quickly, holding up his hand. "My reputation is at stake. Make this bet a big one."

"Go ahead," Jules Kolto whispered. "He did it worse that time than he did before! Did you spot the card!"

"Sure!" Bug Eye answered in an undertone! I got it cold. Oh, won't Pop be ravin' when he wakes up! All right, Frisco," he added loudly. "I'll take you on. Here's twenty-five berries." He pulled a roll from his pocket. "I'm puttin' it all on the middle card."

Pop gazed at the money a moment. At first Roy thought he hadn't enough with him to cover it, and was about to step forward when Teddy pulled him back.

"Wait till the end," he suggested.

"But I hate to see Bug Eye skin Pop that way," Roy objected. "It isn't right."

"He's going to give it all back," Teddy declared. "He said so. He just wants to have the laugh on Pop. Even so, I feel kinda sorry for the old bird. He doesn't know what it's all about. I never saw that trick done more clumsily than the way he just did it. The ace of spades is right in the middle.''

Pop had his hand in his pocket now, and drew out a wad of bills.

"Care to make it fifty, stranger?" he asked carelessly, looking at Bug Eye."

"You bet!" the puncher replied, and added some more money to the pile. "There you are. Fifty smackers.''

Placidly Pop tossed a wad of bills on the bench. "Turn 'er over," he said laconically.

Bug Eye reached out his hand. He rested it on the middle card, then, suddenly, he turned it face up.

His neck craned forward.

Then he gave a gasp of dismay, and started back. A laugh, low at first, then growing into a roar of mirth, arose from the spectators. Pop stretched a hand for the money.

The card Bug Eye had turned up was neither the ace of spades, of diamonds nor of hearts— but the joker!

CHAPTER V

A Startling Cry

The effect of Pop Burns' duplicity on Bug
Eye was to make the voluble puncher more
than ever distrustful of human nature. It was
obvious to all that Pop and Jules Kolto had
cooked up the scheme between them. Pop was
really good at the game known as three-card
monte, and when Bug Eye began to spout
about his new accomplishment the members of
the X Bar X determined to give him a ride on
something besides a bronco.

Pop did give the fifty dollars back, but along
with it he delivered a lecture to Bug Eye that
almost made the cowboy wish Pop had kept the
fifty *and* the sermon. For ten minutes, by the
clock, Pop talked on the wickedness of the
present generation, the while holding the roll
of bills in one hand and using them forcibly to
demonstrate his points. The moon shone on a
crestfallen bronco-buster as Pop concluded his
speech and handed the money over with a part-
ing word of advice.

Bug Eye took the roll silently and walked
into the bunkhouse. The punchers waited for a

moment. They were rewarded by beholding a
small object about six inches square come sailing out into the night. Teddy sauntered over
to where it had fallen and picked it up. It was
a book—a book with one word of its title underscored by the simple method of drawing a
gun-sight below it. The title was "Hypnotism.
Its Use and Abuse." The word underscored
was *abuse*.

It was late at night when Teddy and Roy
left the bunkhouse and sought their beds.
There had been much talk—mostly, of course,
of the success of Pop's trick. For a while Bug
Eye assumed an injured air, but a nature such
as his is never long in dismay. He was soon
laughing with the rest.

Teddy said nothing of the ape he and Roy
had encountered. He realized it would be
equivalent to reading Cicero to a crowd at a
football game. The punchers were in that mood
which frequently comes upon men who are more
than half boys, a mood which will take a serious statement and turn it into a joke. Pop was
in rare form, and Teddy hardly relished having his story picked apart by the veteran
puncher and laid open to the jeers of a raucous
audience.

At the breakfast table the next morning, Mr.
Manley suggested that Nell, Ethel, Belle Ada
and the two boys ride down the river a way,
have lunch there, and fish.

"Haven't had a mess of trout in a good while," the boss of the X Bar X declared. "Want to try it, boys?"

"Sure do! Nothing around here that needs our attention?" Roy questioned.

It was Mr. Manley's idea to invest his sons with responsibility as early in life as possible, and to this end he had arranged a plan whereby each was to have the management of the ranch on alternate weeks. Of course he still retained his position as "official overseer," but, in effect, Teddy and Roy were alternately managers of the X Bar X.

"You can take the day off," Mr. Manley replied to his son's question. "I'll appoint you on the entertainment committee," and he grinned. "Will they serve, girls?"

"Oh, of course—" Nell started, when Belle Ada interrupted.

"It might help if they knew some card tricks," and she nodded solemnly. "Card tricks help to while away the time. Ask Bug Eye."

"So you heard about it, too, Miss Gossip?" Teddy remarked. "There isn't much that happens around here that you don't get in on, is there?"

"Not much," came in a decided tone. "Nor there won't be, either."

"Why that last remark, sister mine?" Teddy asked, approaching and casually seizing a braid

of the girl's black hair. Roy intervened in time
to save a dish of cereal from mingling its con-
tents with the design on the rug. The contest
was declared a draw.

Before they started for the river, Roy had a
talk with Nick. He thought it best to be frank
with the puncher, for they were friends of old
standing, and Roy wanted to be in a position
to help the cowboy if he got the chance. Blunt-
ly he put the question to Nick, asking if he had
been in Los Dipono on business connected with
the legacy he was expecting.

"Yes, Roy, I was," Nick made answer simply. "Los Dipono is my home town. I was
born there. But they won't take my word for
it."

"What do you mean?"

"Well, it seems that the law won't believe
a man's born unless he's got a paper to prove
it. That's my case. My uncle died about six
years ago an' his will just turned up. Seems
he left it stickin' in the coffee grinder in the
kitchen, so he wouldn't forget it. Well, he died
in the night, an' he didn't have his coffee in
the mornin' or maybe he did, but it was ghost
coffee. Well, the will stayed in that grinder
until a few weeks ago, when the old house was
sold an' fixed over. They found it then. Seems
Uncle Mike had a bank account of some six
thousand dollars, an' he left it all to me, 'cause
I was his nearest livin' relative."

"Why, that's fine, Nick! Six thousand dollars! When do you get it?"

"Yea, that's fine, but it ain't so simple as it looks." Nick rolled a cigarette deftly and stuck it in the corner of his mouth. "To get the dough I got to prove I'm born."

"You've got to have a birth certificate?"

"Somethin' like that. Snakes! Twenty-seven years ago they didn't know what them things was in Los Dipono. You know what the town is like now. You can imagine what it was then."

Roy thrust his hands deep in his pockets and thought.

"Isn't there any other way you can prove who you are?"

"Outside of takin' the judge on for a couple of rounds, I don't see how. I'm waitin', hopin' those fool lawyers can see daylight without havin' it pointed out to 'em. Trouble is, there's always flies where there's honey."

"Some one else trying to get the money?"

"You bet! Feller turned up who says he's me—but I know he ain't. Until one of us can prove who we are, the money stays put."

"Got any ideas?"

"Plenty, but they don't amount to much. There's Belle yellin' for you. We'll talk when you get back. Good luck—hope you get lots of fish."

Nick Looker turned and walked towards the horse corral. As soon as he was out of sight of the boys his face took on an anxious look.

"Jumpin' bugs, if I don't get the money I will sure be in a hole," he muttered to himself. "What will Ham say when he comes back —and what will the whole bunch say when they find it out?"

Nick Looker had not told Teddy and Roy the whole of his troubles—how another cowboy named Ham Kidder, had gone on a trip into Mexico with two Mexicans. Ham had just gotten a windfall of six hundred dollars and, not liking the appearance of the men, had turned over the six hundred to Nick for safe keeping. Nick had carried the roll of bankbills with him when riding cattle and one night, in a fierce wind and rain storm, the roll of money had disappeared. The cowboy had looked all over for it but without avail.

At first Nick had been much alarmed for Ham was a good friend and he knew the loss must be made good. Then had come the news of his uncle's death and at once Nick had told himself he could pay Ham his six hundred out of that. He didn't care much for money himself. But he wanted to square up—so that nobody would think he was a thief and had gambled away the roll.

Roy joined the others who were waiting for him with saddled horses and picnic baskets already prepared. They struck directly for the river, intending to follow it until they came to a good place to camp.

Belle told them she had placed the stuffed bear which Teddy had brought her on the ground near the house just when Pop was approaching, and the old puncher had run forward to catch it before it escaped.

"You should have seen his face when he found out it wasn't real!" the girl laughed. "Wasn't it funny Ethel? Pop said he never saw a bear done so well before. He meant stuffed, I guess. I told him an old man in Dipono did it, and he was anxious to know his name. Said he wanted an egg stuffed that Sing Lung served for breakfast the other day, so that it would be preserved for future generations as a relic."

"You heard about Bug Eye and his hypnotism, didn't you?" Teddy asked Nell and Ethel.

"Belle told us," Ethel answered. "I do wish we had been there! Poor Bug Eye! He always loses, no matter what happens. His Fishmobile broke down the other day, and he says he can't fix it. Uncle Peter offered to buy it from him for junk, but Bug Eye wouldn't sell."

By this time they had reached the river, and decided to take the left trail.

"Little different from the last time we started up here," Roy remarked. "Just about here is where we launched the canoe. Remember, Teddy? And we didn't know whether it was going to leak or not. Thank goodness it didn't.''

"I certainly do remember,'' Teddy responded. "You don't forget a trip like that very soon. But it was worth it—in fact, I'd do it all over again just to see Gus walk in once more and say: 'Boys, meet the wife!' Wasn't that rare? Snakes, that sun is getting hot! Anybody want a drink of water?''

He held his canteen up, and both Belle and Ethel took advantage of the offer. They rode on then until nearly eleven o'clock, when they came to a small cove set back among lush willows. The vegetation here was vividly green, almost sparkling. There was a freshness about the place, as though it had been blown clean of any unusual motion and strife. Without a word the riders headed in and dismounted.

The horses were picketed up the stream a way, and Teddy and Roy prepared their fish-lines. The rods were joined together, the flies selected, and the casting started.

It was Belle Manley's boast that she could do anything her brothers did, and, in truth, she succeeded passably in most of her undertakings. But as neither of the girls from the East had ever tried fly fishing, she had left her rod at home. So she, Ethel and Nell now threw themselves under the shade of a tree to wait until the boys tired of their sport and demanded lunch. But casting is a fascinating diversion, and an hour passed before either of the brothers showed signs of waning interest. They were some distance downstream now, around a bend and out of sight of the girls.

There had been several strikes, but luck was against them, and the fish had all gotten away. But now Roy's rod bent in a sudden bow, and the reel sang a mad song as the line played out.

"Got him!" he called, and snapped on the brake.

At that moment a scream, high, distinct and terror-stricken, winged down to the boys. It came from the place where they had left the girls.

CHAPTER VI

STARTING A CHASE

ROY'S strike was forgotten. The rod was almost torn from his grasp as his hand relaxed, and an expression of fear whitened his face.

"That was Belle's voice!" he whispered hoarsely. He cleared his throat, and leaped up the bank. Then he realized that he still held the fishing rod, and savagely he snapped the line and threw the rod on the ground.

Teddy was directly behind him. He, too, cast his rod from him and set out with a single purpose in mind—to reach the girls as soon as possible.

Madly the two boys raced around the bend. There were no more screams, but the very silence was frightening. What could have happened?

They came in sight of the cove.

"Thank heaven!" Teddy breathed, and in a moment was comforting a tearful, excited girl, who clung to him desperately.

"All right, sis," the boy soothed. "Take it easy, now! Why did you yell? What's the matter?"

47

Nell and Ethel were trembling, but were able to talk coherently. Nell turned to Roy.

"She—Belle—saw the gorilla," she stammered.

"The gorilla!" Roy started back in horror. "Here? When? Tell me—"

"I was walking down that way," Belle sobbed, then stopped. "Teddy, you can let go of me now. I'm all right." She took a deep breath. "I'm not usually like this," and she smiled slightly toward Nell and Ethel. "You must think I'm an awful coward! But if you 1ad seen—" she shuddered, then raised her head proudly. "But I didn't run from him! I just stood there—and looked at him!"

"Belle, start from the beginning!" Roy said sharply. "Did you see an animal?"

"I saw the gorilla that Teddy told us about!"

Roy bent casually down and picked up a heavy stick. He noticed that Teddy did the same.

"I walked down that trail," Belle continued, her voice stronger now. "I wanted to pick some water-cress for our lunch. Nell and Ethel were waiting here. I was just about to call to them to come with me, when—when it happened! A big ape jumped right in front of me—as near to me as you are, Teddy!" She trembled violently, but managed to go on. "His arms touched the ground, they were so long. He stood and glared at me—and I stood and glared back! I don't know how long he stayed there, but finally he ran, almost like a man. Then I screamed!"

"We heard you!" Teddy exclaimed. "Roy, let's look into this." He resolutely started for the trail.

"No, Teddy! No!" Belle cried, seizing his arm. "Please don't! Stay here—with us!"

"We'd better, Teddy," Roy said quietly, glancing quickly at his brother. "We'll never find him now. He's probably away off by this time. Come on, let's eat."

"We're—going to stay *here?*" Ethel asked, in surprise.

"Do you want to go home?" Teddy countered.

The girl hesitated, looked at the others, and then shook her head.

"I'm game," she said grimly. "If Belle can stand it, I can."

"Don't worry about me," Belle said. "If I left now I should be a coward. Do you really think there's danger, Roy?"

Her brother considered for a moment.

"No, I really don't. We are five, and no such animal I ever heard of would attack a party. Besides, that ape, or whatever it is, is probably tame. He has escaped from some menagerie, I'll bet anything. I don't believe he'd harm anyone. Maybe he just wants company!"

"Well, I wish he'd stick to his own friends,

and not come bothering us!'' Teddy laughed, and shook the stick he held in his hand. ''He won't get a welcome here, anyway!''

''I'll tell a maverick he won't!'' Roy agreed grimly. ''Now let's eat. We'll talk about the gorilla later, if you want to—though I'd just as soon forget him.''

In spite of their fright, the meal was a jolly one, though they went without the water-cress. They sat in a circle in a clearing, so that every side would be guarded, though they did not admit that this was the reason for the arrangement. Gradually they came to look upon their strange visitor as a harmless beast, and simply one to be avoided. Roy's argument that it had escaped from a circus was accepted, and they speculated as to whether there was a reward offered for the animal.

''Be nice to collect it,'' Teddy declared, sinking his teeth into his fourth sandwich. ''But I'll leave the job to some one else. I never was an informer.''

''Goes against your principles, hey, Teddy?'' Roy jeered. ''Well, it does against mine, too! We'll let Mr. Ape alone—for a while, at least. Pass those olives, please, somebody.''

An incident so close to the tragic is not easily forgotten, no matter how studiously mention of it be avoided, and frequently one of them would start at some sound near by. At the conclusion of the meal, Teddy suggested that his and Roy's rods were still where they had left them, and all wandered down to the bank of the stream.

"No use to fish any longer," Roy declared. "My line is broken. If you want to, Teddy, cast some more. Dad is expecting a mess of trout."

"Not to-day, thanks," Teddy answered, taking his rod apart. "We'd better start for home."

No one asked his reason, as they all understood. Teddy and Roy were not frightened, but there were three girls with them. If a wild animal was at large near them, this was no time to hunt it.

The ponies were remounted, the picnic baskets hung on the saddles, and the young folks turned the horses' heads up the river, keeping the broncos close together.

Roy, thinking this was as good a time as any, told his brother of the conversation he had had with Nick and of the inheritance the puncher expected.

"He was born in Los Dipono!" Teddy exclaimed. "I always thought Nick came from Texas. Do you think he can prove who he is?"

"Hope so," Roy replied. "I'd like to see Nick fall into some gravy. He's a real man."

"Did he say what his real name was?" Ethel inquired, her eyes wide.

"Why, Nick Looker!" Roy answered, in surprise. "To be more exact, Nicholas A. Looker.

What made you think it was anything else, Curly?''

Ethel blushed slightly.

''I've always read that in the West men take another name, because—oh, well—''

''Our romancer!'' Teddy laughed. ''Sorry, Curly, but there's no mystery here. Nick Looker is his real name. If a man changes his title he usually has some good reason, like The Pup. Is that the reason you thought Nick was in disguise?''

''Maybe,'' Ethel laughed. ''He's just plain Nick, then?''

''Well, he's not so plain—he was born on Christmas Day. That's one of the things he wants to prove—his birthplace and the date. He's going to have a mean job on his hands to do it, too. There seems to have been no record kept of his arrival, and he can't find anyone who can testify that he is as he claims. I sure hope he makes out.''

They rode along some distance in silence. There was much to think about, and the scare Belle had received put rather a damper on the party. They came to the spot where they were to turn off, and Roy was about to make a remark when Teddy rode close to him and seized his arm.

''Some one in a hurry,'' he declared in a low voice. ''Look.''

A rider was hastening toward them. At first

they could not make out who he was, but as he came closer Belle exclaimed;

"It's Nat Raymond. Do you suppose he wants us?"

"Soon know," Roy replied. "Hey, Nat! What's the rush?"

The rider waved his hand, and pulled his pony to a sliding stop.

"After somebody," he panted. "See anyone come this way?"

"No, we didn't," Teddy answered, looking at Nat in surprise. "What happened?"

"Can't tell yet," Nat answered, breathing hard. "But I was ridin' toward home—been over to the north fence—an' I seen three men actin' funny. I don't mean standin' on their heads, neither! They was bendin' over a fire, an' one of them was holdin' somethin' in his hand. Thinks I, they ain't the kind to toast marshmallows, so I'll have a look. They're on our land, anyway. So over I rides, but as soon as they spotted me they kicked the fire out, hopped on their ponies, an' beat it. I chases 'em for a ways, but lost 'em."

"What did they look like?" Teddy asked, interested.

"Well, one of 'em was an undersized runt who seemed like as if he ever spoke it 'ud be in a high voice, like a girl. Don't know why I got that idea, but I did. The others were just ordinary punchers."

"An undersized runt," Roy mused. "High voice—jimminy, Teddy, could it have been Denver Smith?"

"Denver Smith—the bird who tried to get away with our cattle on Whirlpool River!" cried Teddy. "If it was—Nat, you go ahead! See what you can make out of this! Roy and I will get off home and tell dad, and follow you. Let's go! Come on, Belle—step on it! Sorry to interrupt your picnic, girls, but this is business! So long, Nat. Ride 'em down if you can!"

CHAPTER VII

THE HOLD-UP

"THERE goes the picnic," Belle called to Ethel, as she rode along behind Teddy. "Something always happens when we start out."

Ethel laughed, and urged her horse to a better speed. Teddy and Roy were intent on just one thing—getting home and spreading the alarm.

It was important that Denver Smith be brought to justice, for while he was at large the community was in constant danger of depredations. The cattlemen of this day depend not so much on their own successful pursuit and capture of rustlers and other thieves as they do on the established law. Frequently the law lets them down—hard.

Denver Smith, now cattle thief, once second-story and confidence man in the East, was wise enough to profit by this false security the ranch owners felt. In this section of the country a sheriff was appointed, not elected. It was a political job solely, and for that reason the incumbent was often lax in running down evil-doers.

When Teddy and Roy reached the ranch they found their father about to ride to Eagles, a town about ten miles from the X Bar X. In a few sentences they told him of Nat Raymond's discovery.

"You want to ride after 'em?" Mr. Manley asked, looking quizzically at his sons.

"Sure! Don't you? Maybe we can catch 'em!" Teddy exclaimed. He glanced at his father. "Wouldn't you like to see Denver Smith in jail, Dad?"

"Yep," Mr. Manley answered laconically, pulling out his corncob pipe. "If he'd only stay there. Now listen, boys. What chance do you think you've got of roundin' up three men who may be any place at all by this time? Furthermore, are you sure it was Denver Smith?"

"Well, not exactly," Roy replied dubiously. "Nat said one of them was a little runt who looked as though he might have a high-pitched voice—"

Mr. Manley let out a roar of laughter and clapped his son on the back.

"Roy, I thought you were so careful about lookin' before you jumped!" he snickered. "Tell me, now—do you really think you have a Chinaman's chance of roundin' up Denver Smith?"

Roy glanced at the ground and smiled sheepishly.

"You're right, Dad," he declared. "We

haven't. Guess I was kind of excited. Well, we'll let Nat have the fun alone. But I'd have thought Nat was usually pretty leary about following false leads, too.''

"Who, Nat Raymond?" Teddy asked. "Not him! He's as bad as any of us. Pop, now—he's different. He'd want a map and compass before he'd take a flier at chasing anyone. All right, Dad, we'll call it off."

Belle, who, together with Ethel and Nell, was standing a little apart, came forward.

"Aren't they going after the rustlers?" she asked.

"No, we aren't," Teddy answered, grinning widely.

"And we rode all that distance as fast as we could go for nothing! Roy, I thought better of you. I am disappointed." And she pretended to turn aside in dismay.

"Aw, cut it out," Roy grumbled. "I should have known better, I'll admit it. Guess I'm due for a little roasting."

"Ah, Roy, you know we don't mean it," Belle said in exaggerated solicitude, taking her brother's hand. "Come over here and console him, girls. Poor Roy!"

"Not much," Roy yelled, vaulting into the saddle again. "Pick on Teddy! He's nearest! Me, I have business!"

"You had him all fussed up, Belle," Teddy laughed, as he watched his brother ride away.

"You shouldn't have brought in Nell and Ethel, then he'd have been all right. Never knew he was so bashful. He's a year older than I am, and yet—"

"And yet," Ethel said demurely, but with a mischievous twinkle in her eyes, "you're quite the man of the world, aren't you?" She moved closer to Teddy. "Big strong hero from the great open spaces, will you be my valentine?" She seized Teddy's hand and gazed innocently into his eyes.

Whatever else Eastern girls may be lacking in, they are not deficient in the art of fascination. Teddy blushed, coughed, and shuffled his feet.

"Hope it—hope it doesn't rain," he murmured.

"Our polished man of the world hopes it doesn't rain!" Mr. Manley roared. He had been watching the little byplay with amused eyes. "Can't you think of anything better to say to her than that, Teddy?"

"Aw, Dad, have a heart," Teddy muttered, red to the ears. "I must find Roy—want to tell him something. See you later."

He discovered that Ethel still held his hand and that unless he dragged it away rudely he would have to remain standing there until she released him. He coughed again, and looked at Belle.

"Hot," he said in a low voice. "Say, er—

Ethel, would you like to come with me? We can—"

"Don't bother," Ethel replied, her laughter ringing out clear. "There!" She released his hand. "Is that what was bothering you? Good-bye, Teddy—see you soon!"

"You bet!" Teddy yelled, springing into the saddle. "And the next time I won't be in such a hurry to leave, either!"

"All he needs is a bronc under him an' he'd defy anyone," Mr. Manley chuckled. "On the ground he's like a fish out of water. I'll bet if you tried that while he was mounted, Curly, he wouldn't have run like that!"

"Well, maybe I'll try it some day," Ethel said, as she laughed. "I just wanted to show him Roy wasn't the only one who was bashful. But—I like bashful boys," and she turned and watched the upright figure of Teddy as he rode along.

"You don't say!" Nell laughed, pinching her cousin's arm. "Well, Teddy will have to hear about that!"

"Don't you dare!" Ethel murmured, blushing furiously. "Nell Willis, if you do, I'll—"

Whatever she would have done was never threatened, for at that moment Nat Raymond rode into the yard. Mr. Manley walked forward to meet him, and the girls went into the house.

"Boss," Nat started, "I saw—"

"I know you did," Mr. Manley interrupted. "Did you catch 'em?"

"Naw," Nat uttered in a disgusted voice. "Never saw 'em again. Where's Teddy an' Roy, boss?"

"Around somewhere. I told 'em not to bother chasin' somebody they didn't have a China-man's chance of gettin'."

"More truth than poetry in that, boss. Glad they didn't. It may not have been Denver Smith at all—in fact, I wasn't even thinkin' of Denver when I started chasin' 'em. I just wanted to keep 'em off our land an' show 'em we didn't want no fires built near our fences."

"You did right," Mr. Manley approved. "We can't afford to have strangers sneakin' near our cattle after all the trouble we had with rustlers. Say, if you see those youngsters of mine tell 'em I want 'em, will you? I'm ex-pectin' a package by express, an' I want 'em to ride over an' bring it in."

Nat nodded, and spun his horse around. He found Teddy and Roy in conversation near the corral, and gave them their father's message. Then he told them of his unsuccessful pursuit.

"I rode up that stream till she curved—by the cove, you know—but I never seen hide nor hair of 'em. They must have taken a side trail. So I moseyed back to the ranch, hopin' I'd catch you-all before you left."

"Didn't see anything else by the cove, did you?" Roy asked.

"What d'ye mean—anything else?"

"Well, any animal—or queer looking man."

"Nope," Nat answered, in surprise. "Nary a thing. Got a reason for askin'?"

"We saw some kind of a big animal while we were there—" Teddy spoke quickly—"and Roy just wondered if you'd come across it. But never mind. Come on, Roy—let's be going."

As they rode away, Teddy suggested in a low voice to his brother that it would be a waste of words to tell Nat of the gorilla.

Roy agreed with him. A little later found the two boys riding toward Eagles with orders to bring back a small package from the express office.

The boys rode fast to reach Eagles and return before night. On their way they stopped at Bitter Cliff Lookout for a moment, to get the view, but they had no time to give to sightseeing, and soon rode on again. Both boys recalled the time that they had first met Nell Willis and Ethel Carew. They had come over this same route, but in an auto that time, for their horses had been stolen.

"Nell and Curly thought it was their fault when these broncs were rustled," Teddy chuckled. "And remember how they screamed when Bug Eye drove 'em round Bitter Cliff?"

"I'll tell a maverick I do!" Roy answered.
"But they sure got on to the West quickly.
Takes more than a high cliff to make 'em yell
now."

They came to Eagles and rode down the main
street. Teddy dismounted and went into the
railroad station, while Roy waited. He returned in a moment with the package.

"Want to start right back?" he asked Roy.

"Might as well. Unless you have something
you want to do."

"How's yore dad, boys?" came a voice, and
Hank Foley, the ticket agent, rolled toward
them. "Rolled" is the only word to express his
gait. He seemed to proceed as a carriage wheel
might with the felly removed and the spokes
touching the ground. True, Hank had only two
spokes, his legs, but the effect was the same.

"He's jake, thanks," Teddy replied. "How
you been?"

"Oh, fair to middlin'. My arm hurts me
some, come damp weather. But I shouldn't
complain. Say, I hear tell Nick Looker is due
to fall into some money."

"Is he?" Roy opened his eyes wide. How
did Hank know about it?

"Heard two fellers talkin' about it yesterday in the station. Well, I hope he gets it. I
like Nick. What under the sun—"

The exclamation caused Teddy and Roy to
whirl about to face in the direction Hank was

staring. Then they saw the reason for his sudden remark.

Down the street a short distance was a bank. Not a very large bank, to be sure, but still a bank, and the pride of Eagles. It was a brown stone structure, one story high.

Running from the bank were two men with masks on and with guns in their hands, looking behind them as they ran. There was a quick report. One of the men had fired.

CHAPTER VIII

MOVIE FOLK

ROY MANLEY leaped from his horse. Teddy rushed forward, followed by Hank Foley.

"Watch it, Teddy!" Roy yelled. "Don't jump 'em! You haven't got a—"

"They ain't got no broncs," Hank panted. "We can get 'em if they—"

"Hey, you guys!" a voice boomed, "stay out o' focus. Stay out! Oh, monkeys, they're in! All right, don't cut, you ninny—take it! take it! Don't cut! Point your guns at 'em, boys! That's it! Now back away, you guys! That's it —back away! More—all right—fine! Now cut!"

A florid-faced man who had been concealed behind a small shack stepped forward, mopping his face with a handkerchief.

"Pretty near spoiled, but I guess she came out O. K. Lucky you guys realized it was a picture."

"A—a picture?" Teddy stammered. Then he saw that a large camera was set up across the street from the bank. The camera man was fussing with a small lever on the side of the machine. Understanding came quickly.

"They were taking a movie!" Roy exclaimed, and a grin broke over his face. "And we're in it."

"Hey?" Hank exploded, and came to a dead stop, a look of amazement on his features. "No hold-up? What in the name of seven kinds of—"

"Sure, it's a movie!" Teddy declared. The "robbers" had now removed their masks and were coming forward. One of them, the taller, laughed good-naturedly.

"Figure we were sticking up the bank?" he asked pleasantly. "This was just a scene. And it looks like you fellows were in it, too. Added a little local color."

His companion, a young chap with a bored look on his face, muttered something about "country hicks," and turned aside. The tall man winked at the boys.

"He's got the high-hat complex," he whispered as he grinned. "Sam, did you get enough footage on it?" he added turning to the director.

"Expect so," the florid-faced man grunted. "Lem, how much?"

"One-sixty," the camera man answered, looking at a register on his machine.

"Plenty. Sorry you boys were made actors without your consent, but I guess you won't mind. Expect I'd better introduce myself. I'm Tod Jackson."

"Tod Jackson!" Roy exclaimed. "I've seen your pictures, Mr. Jackson. I'm glad to meet you. My name's Roy Manley, and this is my brother Teddy. Hank Foley on your left."

The actor thrust out his hand.

"Glad to know you all," he grinned.

Hank took the proffered hand with a look of awe. "Yo're Tod Jackson?" He muttered. "Well, well, well. Er—I mean—well, well."

"Not at all," Tod laughed. "Think nothing of it. I'd introduce you to the other member of the cast, but he seems to have disappeared." He winked again.

"Who is the other actor?" Teddy asked. From the way the younger lad had bolted, Teddy thought he might have even greater claim to fame than did Tod Jackson.

"He's a new man," Tod answered. "Just trying him out. He hates anyone to horn in on the footage he's supposed to have. Say—" a sudden thought struck him. "You boys on a ranch around here?"

"Dad owns the X Bar X," Roy answered. "Why?"

"Your father owns a ranch?" Tod Jackson repeated. "I wonder if—hey, Sam, come over here!" Sam waddled forward. "Boys, this is Sam Kane. Sam, like to have you meet Roy and Teddy Manley and, er—"

"Hank Foley," Teddy finished for him. "Glad to know you, Mr. Kane."

"Their father owns a ranch around here," Tod continued. "And I had an idea it might be just what we were looking for."

"Available for location?" the fat man asked laconically.

"Don't get you," Teddy replied, grinning. "You'll have to translate, I'm afraid."

"He means could we use it for some scenes," Tod explained. "Of course, we'd be glad to pay whatever it is worth to you. We're new out here—sent out by the big boss to make Westerns." He didn't tell who the big boss was but Roy gathered that he was the principal director, or possibly the owner, of the company. "We haven't got much of a staff with us—you saw most of 'em. Got an ingenue and a vamp somewhere around—sleeping, I reckon. You'll meet them later."

"A—vamp?" Hank Foley stuttered. "A *real vamp?*"

"Pretty real," Tod laughed. "However, I guess you're safe. But how about that ranch, boys? Think we could arrange it?"

"I'm sure we could," Roy answered warmly. He had taken an immediate liking to Tod Jackson, as had Teddy. "If you care to ride over, I'll introduce you to dad, and you can ask him. But I know it'll be all right."

"Fine! Would it be rushing things if we came this evening?"

"Not at all! Come right along! Tell you how to get there."

"I'll show 'em," Hank broke in eagerly. "I ain't busy this evenin'. You fellers got a car?"

"Yes, we have. That's very nice of you. What time?"

"Right after supper, if that's satisfactory to you," Roy answered.

"Great! Sam, you can come then, can't you? Check! And I'll bring our camera man along, to look over the lay of the land. Well, we'll see you later. So long!"

"So long, Mr. Jackson!"

"Good-bye!"

"He's a mighty nice fellow," Teddy said impulsively, as he remounted his pony. "I like him. Not at all stuck up, is he? I always had the idea movie actors were—well—a trifle blah. Nothing high-hat about him. Wonder if he'll bring the actresses along with him? Golly, won't Belle be excited when we tell her what happened! Let's—"

"Say, hold up a second, will you?" Roy laughed. "You're going like a house afire. Why this sudden rush of language?"

"All right—all right, my bully boy! Make believe you're not up in the air too! Conservative Roy! Be natural, sonny!"

"You win," Roy chuckled. "I'm about as excited as you are. Golly, we were in that picture, weren't we? Maybe we'll get a chance to be in another. If he's going to shoot ranch scenes— yes, I said *shoot*—proper term—then he'll want punchers in it. *That's* our meat! Baby! We'll be wild and woolly cowboys!"

They were riding much faster than they had when they were leaving the X Bar X, for both were anxious to get home and tell the great news. They reached the ranch by six o'clock.

They found Belle Ada and her two friends in the yard.

"Hey, we're actors!" Teddy yelled, springing from his bronco. "We're in the movies!"

"You don't say!" Ethel laughed. "Warm, isn't it?"

"No, that's a fact—we are," Roy declared seriously. "We're in a moving picture."

"Roy Manley, if you don't climb down from that pony and tell us all about it I'll come up there and get you!" Belle exclaimed imperiously. "What movie? What are you talking about?"

So then the tale was told.

"And they're coming over here to see dad about having the ranch for location," Teddy finished.

"Coming over here! When?" Nell asked, her eyes shining.

"To-night! Right after supper. And let me warn you—if you girls get interested in the

actors, Roy and I are going to meet the ingenue
and the vamp. Hey, Roy?"

"I'll tell a maverick!" Roy grinned. "Who
knows—we may turn into movie actors!"

"And you may not!" Belle added grimly.
"We'll see mother about that. Just mention the
word *vamp* to her and see what happens!"

"Guess I won't, thanks," Teddy laughed,
"But wait till you see Tod Jackson! He's as
regular as they come—isn't he, Roy? There's
some chap that plays with him who isn't so
good, but we won't have to bother with him.
There's the supper bell. Let's eat!"

After supper all sat on the porch to await
the arrival of the moving picture people. Mr.
Manley had already said they might use the
ranch in any way they pleased, and Teddy and
Roy were eager to tell the news to Tod Jackson.

"Here they come!" Belle exclaimed, as the
sound of a car was heard. "Let's go out and—
no, let's not. We'll sit here until they walk up.
No, let's go in the house and come out when
they're here—or else—"

"Our ickle sister is all het up," Teddy
laughed, and nudged Roy. "Strange what a
commotion an actor creates in the feminine
breast—a-hem! I said it's strange what a—"

"We heard you," Roy grinned. "It doesn't
get any better, no matter how often you say it.
Hey, Tod!—I mean Mr. Jackson," and he ran

down the steps, not so self-assured himself.
"Welcome to the—" then he stopped, for he
saw that there were two ladies in the car.

"Hello, Mr. Manley!" Tod called, and
alighted.

"Roy, if it's all the same to you, and my
brother is Teddy. C'mere, Teddy, you apple!
What you hiding for?" this last in a sibilant
whisper.

"I'm not hiding, you goof! What made you
say that?" Teddy, as red as a beet, walked forward. "Howdy, Mr. Jackson!"

"Tod," the actor grinned. "Hello, Teddy.
Miss Harper and Miss De Lisle, may I present
the Manley brothers, Teddy and Roy?"

"How do you do," the ladies said, bowing.
The blonde, whom Roy suspected of being the
"ingenue," alighted. "What a quaint place!"
she trilled, in a sugary-sweet voice. "Do you
have—ah, Indians and scorpions out here?"

"Yes, ma'am, and rattlesnakes and lizards
and doodlebugs," Teddy answered promptly.
"Not to mention—"

"Pipe down!" Roy whispered. "She's not
kidding—that's just the way she talks."

"Mr. Foley was very kind to show us the
way," Tod said, turning to the ticket agent,
who sat upright and stiff next to the "vamp."

"Yes, it was easy," Hank said suddenly,
leaning forward, his face breaking into a grin
like a field of ice after a spring thaw. "I liked

to do it, I did. I know the way out here fine. I could find it with my eyes shut, I guess. Or almost. Couldn't I, Teddy? Course the road winds a lot, but I'm used to windin' roads. Always was, from a child. My mother used to say: 'Hank,' she'd say, 'Hank——' "

"Come in and tell us," Roy said kindly, stifling a grin. Hank, on the ride over, was frozen into silence by the presence of a "vamp" next to him, and had suddenly opened the gates of conversation at the sight of a familiar face. But now the gates were closed again, and Hank fell back, gasping for breath. He was shocked at his own daring, and it was some minutes before he could gain enough courage to utter another word. By that time the little party had gone to the parlor, as night was rapidly darkening the ranch outlook.

Belle Ada and her girl visitors were tense with eagerness, nor were Teddy and Roy much less so. None of them had any inkling of what strange events the arrival of the movie folk presaged.

CHAPTER IX

Pop Scores

Introductions were soon completed, and Mr. Manley expressed his willingness to let the picture people use the ranch if they wished.

"We couldn't think of taking anything for it," Mrs. Manley put in. "In fact, it's a pleasure to be able to assist you. It isn't often we get a chance to be in moving pictures," and she smiled.

"Think you could use this little girl?" Mr. Manley asked, throwing his arms about Belle Ada's shoulders. "She's been wantin' to be in the movies for a long time. As a heroine; hey, Belle?"

"Daddy!" Belle exclaimed, blushing. "Of course they couldn't use me. They just want experienced actors!"

"Now, I don't know about that," Tod declared. "If it would be agreeable to you, we could use you all. We've got a scene that calls for a number of extras, and if we could hire you, it would save us a lot of work."

"Hire us!" Ethel gasped. "You mean we'd actually be in the movie, like regular actors?"

73

"Of course!" Tod laughed. "We pay ten dollars a day for all extras. Will you do it?"

"Will we do—" Belle started, then stole a look at her mother. "We'll let you know," she finished weakly. "When are you going to take it?"

"You may say yes, Belle," Mrs. Manley smiled. "I shan't object."

Miss Harper, the "vamp," agreed to show the girls what ther was to the art of "make-up."

"And to-morrow we'll start," Tod said, getting to his feet. "We'll be over bright and early, so as to get the benefit of the best sun. What do you think of this place, Lem?" he asked, turning to the camera man.

"Great," was the answer. "Like to live here."

"I was just thinking that myself," Tod said, and grinned. "If—or rather when—I lose my job in pictures will you give me one out here, Mr. Manley?"

"Come right along!" Mr. Manley boomed. "Glad to have you. Any time at all. But I guess it'll be some time before you'll be out of a job. Pictures go like wildfire."

With Hank Foley again seated between the two actresses, the party left the ranch for Eagles. Nell, Belle, and Ethel stood on the porch and waved farewell.

"To think that we're really going to be in

the movies!" Belle sighed, and turned away. "I've always dreamed about it, but I never thought it would actually come true!"

"Miss Bighit—call for Miss Bighit!" a voice shouted from within the house. It was Mr. Manley. "Come on, Star—time to hit the hay. You have to be up early for that Egyptian scene we're shootin'."

"Oh, Dad, isn't it wonderful?" Belle thrilled, and ran in. It was late that night before slumber came to the excited girl. Had she known it, the others were just as restless—and that included Teddy and Roy.

Of course those at the ranch did not know that the moving picture company was a rather small one and, just now, limited as to capital. As soon as the additional capital that had been promised came in, they would make a much larger "spread." But even as it was, like many a dramatic barn-storming company, they considered it best to put on a "big front." Tod Jackson, already known as an actor, was one of the partners in the new company, "The Marvel Films."

It was no everyday affair to have a moving picture company come to the X Bar X. When the punchers in the bunkhouse heard of it the next morning, they set up shrill yells of delight.

"Oh, boy—I'll bet the hero's got a parcel—sweet sugar cane!"

"An' the vamp—out o' my way there, puncher! I'm headin' north!"

"Do the men use, now, perfume, Teddy?"

"This Tod Jackson doesn't, I know that!" Teddy retorted. "Wait till you see him. He's the real thing. Bet he packs a pretty punch, too—he's got a fine pair of shoulders."

Pop alone said nothing. He sat on the top rail of the corral, dangled his skinny legs, and grunted. Whatever his thoughts were concerning the invasion of the X Bar X by the picture people, he kept them to himself.

At eleven o'clock two cars rolled into the ranch yard. The one contained Tod Jackson and the two actresses. The other held the camera, camera man, and the director.

"Hope we didn't come too early," Tod called out as he alighted.

"Too early?" Roy echoed. "This is afternoon for us! Well, we're all set. What do you want us to do?"

"Which shall we take first, Sam?" Tod asked the director.

"Let's see." The short man gazed about him. "The sun is pretty good. Suppose we shoot one hundred and fourteen. Here's the script."

"I thought directors always roared through megaphones," Nell whispered. "This one even asks questions!"

"Sure! This is real," Roy whispered back.

"I reckon you've been reading books about Hollywood. Wonder what one hundred and fourteen means?"

He soon learned that it indicated a certain scene—one in which a crowd of cowboys were lounging about the yard and the hero, straight from the East, comes and asks for a job.

"Silly as it may seem, I'm the hero," Tod Jackson laughed. "I come on all duked out in Eastern clothes and the punchers make fun of me. Then I prove my mettle—at least, that's what the script says. There seems to be quite a lot of mettle-proving lately; hey Sam? I've had to do it three times in the last six months. Pretty soon there won't be any mettle left to be proved. Well, that's the scene. Can we borrow your men? Of course we'll pay them all."

"Guess they'll be glad to do it," Teddy laughed. "Wait, I'll get 'em."

He walked toward the bunkhouse. In a few moments he returned, followed by the strangest crowd of punchers the sun ever shone on.

They were dressed regardless. Gone were the habiliments of their trade—the leather chaps, the woolen shirts, the vests. Instead they wore "store clothes"—and the store must have been pitched near an insane asylum.

There were checkered suits with checks an inch wide. There were pure white suits—palm beach· with red neckties to set them off. There were green suits—green, with tiny red stripes. That there were nearly two of each was not to be wondered at. The store where they had purchased them had a limited assortment, and they took what they could get. They had decided that they would never all go out at once, hence doubles were not objectionable. But now they were all together—and the ensemble gave the general aspect of a sunset gone crazy.

When Tod saw them he staggered back.

"Who—who are these?" he gasped weakly.

Roy grinned.

"Last night, I could have told you," he chuckled. "They used to be cow-punchers. What they are now, is a problem for greater minds than mine."

Guss Tripp, who appeared to be the leader, stepped stiffly forward.

"Ladies an' gents of the pictures," he began pompously, "I wish to welcome you on behalf of my—er, I wish to behalf you—no, that's wrong—I wish—"

"You must be Cinderella!" Tod Jackson roared. "Buddy, I hope you get your wish—but we're not fairy godmothers! Anyhow, I'm glad to meet you. Shake!"

He thrust out his hand. Gus grasped it with a pleased grin.

"Glad to know you, stranger. Yo're Tod Jackson? An' yore hair ain't marcelled, at that. Scuse me—that slipped out." He flushed, but Tod laughed. "I thought all movie actors—"

"Sure, I know!" Tod answered. "Now introduce me to your buddies."

Each puncher in turn stepped forward, and the introductions were most formally made— not only to Tod Jackson, but to the other members of the cast.

"Now, I hope you won't think I'm being nasty—but do you always wear those clothes?" Tod asked, eying the punchers quizzically.

"No sir!" Gus answered proudly. "We put 'em on special."

"Well—" Tod scarcely knew how to proceed. He did not wish to offend the punchers, and he knew how sensitive men can be. He turned to Teddy.

Teddy nodded.

"Mr. Jackson wants to take a picture of you just as you are when you're working," the boy explained. "Those clothes are great, Gus, but they're not what Mr. Jackson wants."

"We're goin' to be in the pitcher?" Nat Raymond asked, his eyes alight. "Say, what'll we do?"

"Just look natural!" Tod laughed. "We'll wait till you change, boys. Then we'll be ready for our great super-special production," and he winked at Roy.

With a rush the punchers made for the bunkhouse. What a cyclonic change of garments occurred in the shack will never be known, but at all events every man was back within five minutes, dressed in his "everyday" clothes.

"That's the stuff!" Tod called enthusiastically, when he saw them. "Great! They'll do; hey Sam?"

"O. K." Sam grunted. "Now if you boys'll drape yourselves about the landscape—say over near that fence—"

"Fence?" Gus Tripp repeated blankly. "What—" Then understanding came to him. "He means the corral, fellers! Let's mosey over."

"Those two gals gonna be in it?" came from Pop Burns, out of a clear sky.

All turned to him in surprise.

"Well, you old bow-legged bronco-buster!" Gus exclaimed, grinning. "Wants to know if the gals are gonna be in it! Well, boil my liver!"

"Now I think he's just sweet," the "vamp" cooed, a mischievous twinkle in her eyes. She stepped toward Pop. "Would you like me to be in it, mister—er—"

"Call him Pop," Gus snickered.

"Mr. Pop?"

"Now, that's a question," Pop mused, in no way ruffled. He put his hand to his chin, in the attitude of a thinker. There were many disappointed looks from the punchers, who expected Pop to turn red and beat a hasty retreat. But Pop was supreme. "That's a question," he repeated. "Do I have to kiss you?"

A roar of laughter went up.

The actress owned herself beaten. She smiled good-naturedly.

"For that you get a picture of me!" she declared. "There are several people, who think themselves sophisticated, to whom you could give lessons, Mr. Pop." She glanced slyly at Tod, who grinned. "You're a true New Yorker, whether you've ever been there or not. Yes, Pop, I'll be in this picture."

The camera was moved over to the corral. The punchers took the attitudes ordered by the director. Teddy and Roy were not in this "shot," their part coming later, but Belle, Ethel, and Nell were. When all was in readiness Sam called out:

"Now you boys be talking. We won't rehearse this, because there's nothing much to it. Just talk. That's right. Make gestures. Tell about the bull moose—or something—you captured. That's it. All right. Ready? Action! Camera!"

CHAPTER X

Nick Looker II

Whatever Sam may have meant by "action," the punchers had their own ideas on the subject. No sooner had the word passed the director's lips than Nat Raymond left his feet in a perfect dive toward Jules Kolto's knees. Jules went down as though his legs were cut out from under him.

"Hey, what's the idea!" Sam shouted in frantic surprise. "Cut, Lem, cut! For the love of mud! You guys gone crazy? What you roughin' it up for? Who told you to do that! Holy cats! This ain't a football match! Hey, you big boy! What 'ud you jump on your friend like that for? Hey?"

"Who, me?" Nat asked in astonishment, getting to his feet. "Me? Why, I thought you wanted me to. You said 'action,' didn't you?"

"I said—I said *what?*"

"You said 'action.' I hearn yuh!"

"Well, slide my trombone," Sam announced, slowly and deliberately. "So that's what you thought I meant by 'action'! Well, shake my saucers! Listen, buddy," he grew confidential.

82

"By action I didn't mean the ordinary, accepted meaning of the word. You see the term is made up of two syllables—one—" he held up one finger—"act, to be *un*natural, to portray another character, to pretend you are another person. Two—" he held up another finger— "shun, meaning to avoid. Hence the word— *act-shun,* to avoid unnaturalness. Or, be yourself! Have I made myself clear?"

"You mean just go ahead an' make believe nothin' was happenin'?"

"Exactly! Be yourself! Are we all ready now? Remember, no rough stuff. Just sit and talk. Tell jokes, if you want to—I don't care. All set, Lem? Action! Camera!"

This time it went off without a hitch. The punchers, huddled together in a congenial group, talked in low tones as though there were no camera grinding away in front of them. Not a single man looked at the lens.

"Fine! fine!" Sam monotoned. "Keep that up. Miss Manley, you and your friends come on now. Just walk on. That's it. You men get to your feet—no, don't bow! Say 'howdy.' That's it! One of you boys show Miss Manley that mountain over there, as though you were telling her about an approaching storm. Point. That's fine. All right, Lem. That'll do. Cut!"

The camera ceased its grinding. Sam mopped his face.

"Like veterans, hey, Tod?" he said, and

turned to the actor with a grin. "Without a single rehearsal. They'll do, I reckon. Might as well shoot that other scene now, while we have 'em all together. The one where you come on. You get into your clothes, and I'll explain to the boys. We'd better try it over once or twice first, I guess."

Tod Jackson looked at Roy.

"Any place where I can get into these city duds?" And he motioned toward a suitcase he had brought with him.

"Sure! Come up to my room. I'll show you." Roy lead the way to the house.

Sam motioned to the punchers to close around him.

"You and your brother are in this one," he said to Teddy. "That is, if it's O.K.'d by you?"

"Suits me," Teddy grinned. "Spill the dope."

"A New Yorker by instinct," Sam muttered. "All right, boys, here's the dope. We're supposed to be on a ranch. I mean, we're supposed to be where we are. This scene is to be taken near the sleeping quarters."

"Bunkhouse," Teddy corrected, with a smile.

"All right. Bunkhouse, then. Well, all you guys are sitting near the bunkhouse. Teddy, here—that's right isn't it?—Teddy is tellin' you about two strangers he met in town. Says they asked him for a job, and he told 'em to come out here. They ought to be along any minute. He says they're city slickers. Then there's business of you birds laughin' to think what you'll do to the city slickers. Of course Tod Jackson is one of the city fellers, and the other is Looker. He's not here yet. Said he'd drive over later and be here by the time we were ready for him.''

''What did you say his name was?'' Teddy asked, looking at the director queerly.

''Well, he says it's Looker. We picked him up just before we came West. Said he was an actor out of a job and wanted to make the West. When he found out we were headed for Eagles, he said that was just where he wanted to go, and if we'd let him come along and give him a trial, he'd work for nothing until he made good. So we let him trail along. Not much of an actor, but I guess he'll do for the little we need him.''

''So his name's Looker,'' Teddy said musingly. The other punchers kept silent, gazing at Teddy. Nick was not among them, having been sent to town by Mr. Manley. ''Don't know what his first name is, do you?''

''Let's see—he did tell me. Oh, yes—Nicholas. That's it. Nicholas Looker.''

Gus Tripp, who was standing directly behind Teddy, started. ''Now that's right funny,'' he began. '' 'Cause we got a man here—''

Teddy pulled back his elbow sharply and caught Gus full in the ribs.

"That's a queer name," the boy said loudly. Gus gazed at him reproachfully for a moment, then his face cleared and he drew in his breath. "I gotcha, Teddy," he muttered. "I'll pipe down."

"It is a funny name," Sam replied, evidently not hearing Gus's half uttered remark. "Looker said he was born some place out around here, and that was the reason he wanted to come back, to see the home town. But if that bozo was born in the West, I'm an Eskimo. He's a New Yorker from his collar button to his shoes. But that's aside from the question. We're taking pictures, not biographies. Listen—" and he proceeded with the directions.

Teddy scarcely heard him.   Nick Looker! And Nick—their Nick—had said there was another man after the money his uncle had left, trying to prove that he was the heir! Could it be that? It certainly was a possibility. And even more than a possibility, it seemed wholly probable that this actor was the man Nick had spoken of. But how had he got news of the legacy in New York?

There never entered Teddy's head a thought that this man might be the real Nick Looker, whose uncle had died in Los Dipono.   Their Nick could not be anything but what he represented himself to be. Their Nick was a man—not a swindler.

Teddy's musings were interrupted by the return of Tod Jackson, resplendent in a checkered suit and a yellow shirt. He explained later that yellow photographed much better than white.

"Everything set, Sam?" he called out. "Did you tell 'em about the action?"

"Yep! But we can't shoot till Looker comes. He's always late. Don't know what we ever took him on for. We'll try a rehearsal, anyhow. Shift the camera over there, Lem." He pointed to the bunkhouse. "You boys take your places. Roy, I want you to be the one Teddy tells his story to, and you interrupt and ask questions. Tod told you about it, didn't he? All right then. Now we'll try it."

Following the director's orders, the punchers collected near the door of the bunkhouse. This time no pictures were taken, but they went through the scene just as though the camera were clicking. At the last moment Sam decided it would be better for Teddy to ride into the scene and leap off his horse in front of the camera, then tell his story. This was done. When Teddy dashed in on Flash and literally flew from his back, the director and Tod could not resist gasps of admiration.

"He sure can ride," Sam murmured. "Tod, we could use him all the way through this pic-

ture if he'd do it! But we'll ask him later.
"O.K., Teddy," he called out. "That's great.
Now begin jabbering to Roy. Check. And you
ask questions, Roy, while the rest of you men
gather in closer so you can hear too.   Fine.
Now you all laugh, and slap your knees.
That's the stuff.

"Now, Tod, you come on.   As soon as he
gets in focus, boys, you shut up quick, like you
didn't want him to hear what you were saying.
Just keep quiet and look at him. You drop
your suitcase, Tod—" the actor held a suitcase
in his hand—" and ask for a job. That's right.
Ask for the foreman—Roy, you be the foreman. Step forward. Look him over well, as
though you never saw an animal like that before. Then turn to the others an' say something—anything, and turn back quick. Good!

"Teddy, you step behind Tod now, and motion to Roy with your thumb. Right. Now
you nod, Roy. Teddy, walk off. Get that
horse of yours and lead him on. In the mean-
time, Roy, you keep asking Tod questions.
That's it! Now bring the horse on, Teddy.
Tod, you look at it sort of scared, but not too
scared. You nod your head. We'll need a
close-up here, so we'll cut. Fine, boys.
Couldn't have been better. If you do it that
well before the camera you'll sure qualify as
regular actors.

"Where in thunder is Looker?" Sam swung

about in disgust. "Always late! He'd be late for his own funeral. Here he comes!"

A cloud of dust appeared down the road, and in a moment it opened to disclose a flivver. At the wheel was Nick Looker II—the actor. He wore a light gray suit and a Panama hat. A smile, meant no doubt to indicate absolute boredom, curled his lips. He put on the brakes hard, slid a few feet, stopped, pushed back his hat, and drew a cigarette case from his vest pocket.

"Hello," he said casually. Not bothering to see whether anyone answered his greeting or not, he lit the cigarette and stepped to the ground.

"Well, Sam, I'm all ready. Tell Lem to give me lots of footage this time."

"What's the idea of showin' up at this time of day?" Sam said truculently. "Who do you think you are—Nero or Napoleon? Snap into it! We've had a rehearsal already!"

"That so?" the man replied carelessly. "That's nice. Then we're all set. These—er, gentlemen,—" he stressed the last word sarcastically—"are local color, I presume? Very nice—very nice. Well, what are we waiting for?"

"We have been waiting for you," Tod Jackson said quietly. "Boys, this is Nick Looker. He's an *actor*."

The punchers did not get the significance of this last word, for all they heard was the name

—Nick Looker. Several voices arose at once, but Roy, realizing the folly of challenging the man at present, raised his hand.

"Listen, boys," he declared. "We'll do no talking. Get me? Mr. Jackson hasn't any more time to waste. If there's anything you-all want to discuss, we'll do it later."

"But, Roy—" Gus started, then stopped.

"No talking *at all,* Gus," Roy said slowly.

Gus gulped. This was not like Roy. Then suddenly he remembered the poke in the ribs.

"Right, boss," he said quickly, and turning to the others said something in a low tone. Heads nodded. "We're ready now," Gus declared aloud.

"Then let's start," Tod said hurriedly. "O. K., Sam."

Once more the director issued his orders. He told "Nick" to come in with Tod and also ask for a job. Tod was then to ride the horse, to "prove his mettle," and "Nick" was to exit as soon as the horse came on.

"And that's all the footage I get?" the actor asked querulously.

"That's all now. What do you want, the whole reel?"

"Why, these bums here get more than that!"

"Just who do you mean by 'bums'?" Nat Raymond asked in an even voice, and stepped forward. "Would you mind elucidatin'?"

"Wait," Tod said quickly. "I have some-

thing to say to Mr. Looker.'' He glanced at
Sam, who nodded. ''Looker, ever since you
joined this company you have put yourself out
to be as disagreeable as possible. We kept you
on because we had to have another man, and
you were the only one in sight. But now we've
got plenty—and they're better actors than you
ever dreamed of being, even if they never saw
a camera before. That last remark of yours
was very poorly chosen. It lets you out. Beat
it, Looker—and don't come back!''

boys, looks like you were goin' to be actors! Why don't you take a crack at it? Things are slow around here—I can spare you for a while."

"What'll we have to do?" Teddy asked, his eyes shining. A job in the movies!

"Well," Tod answered, "our real reason for coming out here was to take some of our scenes on Big Bison Trail. Don't know exactly where that is, but our location man in New York told us about it. He said it's just what we need. So we came West, with just the little cast you see here, hoping to find enough extras on the way to fill in. As you see, we were pretty lucky, for the extras we got are good—exceedingly good!"

"Spread it thin," Teddy laughed. "Say, Roy, that Big Bison Trail is quite a journey from here, isn't it? Could you spare us that long, Dad?"

"Oh, I guess so," Mr. Manley answered. "The old man isn't a cripple yet—he can still toddle. Sure, go to it, boys. You're due for a vacation, anyhow."

"That's mighty fine of you, Mr. Manley," Tod said warmly. "And I appreciate it. Frankly, Looker, by leaving, did put us in a kind of hole. But it's filled now—and better than Looker ever filled it."

"Did you say Looker?" Mr. Manley inquired in a surprised tone. "Was that the name of

the man who just left? Why, we've got a hand
here by that same name, Nick Looker. He's in
town now. Wonder if this bird could be any
relation to him?''

"No relation, Dad," Teddy said quickly.
"It's a long story. This man claims he's the
person we think our Nick Looker is."

"He does?" Mr. Manley's eyebrows went
up. "What's the idea?"

"Well, Nick—our Nick—is expecting some
money that was left to him by the will of his
uncle," Teddy explained. Then he hesitated.
These people were strangers—would Nick care
to have his business broadcast to them? Then
the boy came to a sudden decision. Tod was
not a stranger—he was now a friend. And,
with help from Roy, the tale of Nick's legacy
was told.

"It seems that your late actor is the man
who is trying to swindle Nick out of his money,"
the boy finished. "That's why he was so
anxious to come to Eagles."

"Well, wash my waistcoat if that ain't a
plot!" Sam exclaimed. "The old razzle-dazzle!
No wonder I didn't like him! And to think he
used *us* as a railroad ticket! Well, burn my
breeches—excuse me, ma'am!"

"Sounds just like Bug Eye," Roy said in an
aside to Teddy. Then aloud, "So that's the
story. It's a toss-up between the two Nick
Lookers as to who gets the money. Of course

we'd like to help our man if we could."

"And so would I," Tod put in. "We'll see if we can't do it, too! Now, if that's over, we'll go on with the picture. Start the fire, Sam."

It was some time, following all the excitement before the punchers could settle down again but, after several attempts, the scene was finally rehearsed to the satisfaction of the director, and then it was "shot." Sam was especially enthusiastic about the acting of Roy and Teddy.

"You're great! You'll go like a million bucks," the stout man said excitedly." Couldn't be more natural! Tod, we're lucky! Now for the pay checks. Ten dollars for each of you —oh, don't worry about taking it, the company's got the money. This doesn't come out of my pockets. Yes, Miss Manley and—er, your two friends, you're in on this too. All right, boys—line up!"

"Jimminy, ten smackies for just that!" Jules Kolto sighed. "Gus, you know where that ten *you* got is goin', don't you?"

"To the wife, I expect," Gus laughed. "You sure got a thrifty sister, Jules!"

"It's a good thing you're not campin' here," Mr. Manley said to Tod, with a grin. "You'd have my ranch disrupted. The boys aren't used to makin' money that easy."

"Too bad Bug Eye isn't here. He likes to make money that-a-way!" Nat Raymond exclaimed, and a laugh went up. Bug Eye's "hypnotism" affair was likely to become part of the history of the X Bar X.

Soon after the "payroll" was distributed Tod and the others left for Eagles. Miss Harper, the "vamp," bid a fond farewell to Pop, promising to send him her picture.

"I'll keep it next to my heart," Pop chuckled. "That is, except when I'm ridin'—cause anything in the back pocket is mighty uncomfortable when yo're forkin' a bronc."

"I'd like to see anyone get the best of that bird in the art of snappy come-backs," Teddy murmured. "Did you get that one, Roy? Bet Miss Harper will remember Pop!"

The two cars rolled out of the yard. On the face of every puncher was an expression of awe, as though he had just stepped out of the presence of a great king. The cowboys stood silently, almost reverently. Some one sighed, then Gus looked down at the toe of his boot, saw a pebble, and kicked it gently. Pop opened his mouth, closed it again, and taking off his hat ran his hand over his bald head. One by one the cowboys turned and made for the bunkhouse. Their great day was over.

"She's goin' to send her picture," Nat muttered. "To Pop, of all people! Now that other little girl—the blonde—kinda took my eye. She didn't say a word the whole time she was here.

Maybe she was bashful. Guess I should 'a' said somethin' to her. Oh, well—''

"What you mumblin' about?" Pop demanded. "Jealous, I suppose! That's just what comes of bein' a man of the world like me. You kids—''

"Aw, we've heard all that before," Jim Casey declared. "Turn the record over. That side's all scratched!"

"I'd like to be in the bunkhouse when the gang hashes things over," Teddy said to Roy, as the two brothers walked toward the corral. "Bet they razz Pop. Say, what do you think about that trip to Big Bison Trail?"

"I'm all for it," Roy answered. "But what interests me now is Nick Looker and his money. Isn't it funny we should run into the very man who's trying to do him out of his inheritance? When Nick comes back we'll have to tell him about it. This so-called actor is no more entitled to that money than I am, and, by golly, we ought to see that he doesn't get it!"

"Now, Roy, you must stay calm in this hot weather," Teddy said in mock solicitude. "Can't let my little brother get worked up over some one else's troubles. But seriously, Roy, you're right. If we can see our way clear to helping Nick we'll sure do it. But at present things are up in the air—we know who this other man is, and we know he's after Nick's money. But that's all."

"Yep, that's all," Roy mused. "Seems a shame to sit quiet and let that fake actor get away with pretending he's Nick Looker. Say, it's a good thing Nick is in town, Teddy—suppose he'd been here when that actor came on the scene and was introduced as Nicholas Looker? There'd have been something doing then, by jinks! The way it stands now I doubt whether the actor knows we're on to his graft. It's better that way—we have more chance to beat him to it. As soon as Nick comes—"

"Who in thunderation is this—Bug Eye?" Teddy interrupted, pointing down the road. A car was catapulting toward them, swaying from side to side, the wheels churning the dust up in great clouds. "Sure drives like him! No, it's not either—"

The auto careened into the yard. From the seat sprang a young man whom the boys had never seen before. He had brick-red hair, and even at that distance the freckles on his face stood out plainly. His blue shirt, open at the neck, disclosed an unusually large Adam's apple. The best word to describe his figure, so Teddy Manley said later, was "rangy." The sleeves of his coat were fully two inches too short for the length of his arms.

As he saw Teddy and Roy he bounded forward.

"Am I in time?" he panted. "Are they gone?"

"Is who gone?" Roy asked in surprise. "Take it easy now, and—"

"I can't afford to take it easy!" the youth exclaimed frantically. "That's just the trouble! I've been taking it too easy all the time! Now I've got to wake up! But tell me, for Pete's sake, have they gone? Tod Jackson and the others!"

"Oh, the moving picture people! Yes, they left not ten minutes ago. You just missed them."

With a groan the youth's excitement subsided.

"All that way for nothing!" he muttered. "Now Tod will be sore. But I couldn't help it—that's all there is to it. Those blame monks are more bother than they're worth." The youth sighed deeply. Then he spoke again, and all the bitterness of the world seemed to hang on the words:

"A malediction on all monkeys!"

CHAPTER XII

A Tale of the Ape

Teddy and Roy Manley looked at each other with a definite question in their eyes. The question was: "Is he crazy?"

"Suppose you tell us about it," Roy said soothingly. "The sun's pretty hot. If you'd just step into the shade now—"

"I haven't got time to step into the shade!" this strange young man continued. "I'm late now! All the things that have happened to me! Well, they say it never rains but it pours. First I lose my ticket an' have to waste all that time gettin' another. Then the railroad kicks at transportin' a monkey. Finally I get 'em to agree, bring the monk all the way out here, an', by Murphy, if he don't escape an' I haven't seen him from that day to this! Woosh!"

Teddy was fascinated by the movements of the young man's Adam's apple. As he talked it bobbed up and down at a surprising rate, and once Teddy was sure he saw it describe a complete circle.

"Did you say something about a monkey?"

101

Roy asked tensely. He stared at the red-haired boy.

"I sure did! I put every cent I had into that monk. And then he ups and beats it. Oh, well, that's just another break. I ought to be used to hard luck now." He laughed mirthlessly. "Trouble is, I waste too much time. I'm wastin' it now. But what of it? Pardon me for sittin' down." He dropped on a low bench that stood near the corral, and pulling out a cigarette he applied a match to it and inhaled deeply. "Boy, it's great out here," he said fervently. "Glad I came, even if I did lose the monk."

"Say, listen!" Teddy exclaimed suddenly. "What kind of a monkey was it?"

"Baboon. Almost as large as a gorilla. I was goin' to bring him out here an' rent him to Tod Jackson to use in the movies. Aw, what's the use of talkin'? He's gone—so's my money. So long, mazuma!" He waved one hand carelessly.

"We saw your ape," Roy declared grimly. "We thought he was a gorilla."

"What? You saw him?" The boy leaped to his feet. "Where? When? By Murphy, maybe I'll get him back after all! Tell me about it!"

"Some days ago my brother and I—my name is Roy Manley, by the way, and this is my brother Teddy—some days ago we got caught in a storm over near Sanborn's Point. We headed for a cabin and when we found it this ape of yours had already taken up quarters there. When we went in he came out. Then later—"

"But where did the monk go?" the boy demanded. "Why didn't you stop him? By Murphy, to think he was that close!"

"We were doing no stopping of apes like that," Teddy laughed shortly. "When an ape as big as that one asks to be excused, I always agree—always!"

"Aw, he wouldn't hurt a fly," Brick-top sighed. "Well, never mind. I'm glad you told me. Maybe I can find him. Maybe I could get up a searching party, and—" he looked inquiringly at the two boys. "First, I'd better introduce myself. My card." He handed over the card with a flourish.

Teddy and Roy read the name "Barton O'Day." Underneath in a smaller type were the words, "Specialist in Pithicanthropy."

"Made that up myself," O'Day declared proudly. "Means something to do with monkeys—don't know exactly what. You see I make a living—that is sometimes—by supplying monkeys to moving picture companies, circuses, and the et cetera. This monk that got away from me was my latest venture. I sunk all I had in it, because I heard from some one in the know—' he hesitated for a moment to give emphasis, then repeated—"from some one in the know that Marvel Films—that's the bunch Tod Jackson is with—I know Tod very well—let's see, now—oh, yes—I heard that Marvel Films was in need of a monk. Course they couldn't get one out here, so, thinks I, I'll bring one on and rent it. At Eagles—there's a town for you!—they told me Jackson and the gang were over here. So out I come—to find 'em gone. I'm too slow, I reckon. Always was!" He relayed himself again to the bench, leaned back, caught himself just in time to prevent a fall, and grinned in friendly fashion.

It was impossible to be serious with this youth with the red hair and bobbing Adam's apple, and both Teddy and Roy found themselves laughing in sympathy.

"So that was your monkey," Teddy chuckled. "Well, O'Day, he scared me out of a week's growth. But I'm glad the mystery is cleared up. He's harmless, you say?"

"Absolutely. He's just like a big kid. Likes petting. Say, I'm thirsty."

Teddy led the way into the house and gave O'Day some water. Although he knew it was rude to stare, Teddy could not resist the temptation to watch that Adam's apple perform seemingly impossible feats as the youth drank. When he had finished he sighed deeply and turned toward the door.

"Where you bound for?" Roy asked.

"Who—me? 'Tis a mooted question. I thought maybe I could get a job with Tod—doin' something. Guess I'll look him up in Eagles now. After that—who knows?" He spread his hands in an expressive gesture, meant perhaps to be Latin, but due to the fact that it made his large fists protrude farther than ever from his cuffs, it failed to be anything but comical.

"Well, if you just want a job we might be able to fix you up," Roy suggested. "Can you ride?"

"Subway trains and busses, that's about all. Nope, I wasn't cut out to be a rancher, more's the pity." He sighed again. "But thanks just the same. Guess I'll try my luck with Tod. By Murphy, if I could find the monk—"

He walked down the steps, unconsciously taking them two at a time. Teddy and Roy followed him, supressing grins. Every movement of the tall, lanky youth was strangely grotesque, and there came to the minds of the boys the thought that here, before them, was a natural comedian. Roy resolved to bring Tod Jackson's attention to this as soon as he saw the actor.

O'Day climbed into his flivver, sighed again, stepped on the self-starter, and waved to the boys.

"Thanks, fellows," he called. I'll see you again, I got a hunch. And if you see my monk any place, save him for me. So long."

"So long, O'Day," Teddy answered. "Wish you luck!"

"Call me Break—that's my nickname! Ought to be Bad Break, I guess. Well, see you anon. So long!"

"Break," Roy muttered, as the car shot down the ride. "That's a funny one. Break—oh, sure! Break O'Day! Get it? Golly, Teddy, wasn't he a sketch! So it was his monk that scared us. You know, I like that red-head. Hope he makes out with Tod."

The rest of the day passed uneventfully, but it was hard for Teddy and Roy to resign themselves to the prosaic jobs of ranch life after the events of the morning. Nick Looker showed up at three o'clock, and the boys told him of their discovery.

The puncher expressed concern when he was informed that the man who claimed to be Nick Looker was in the vicinity. Teddy said the actor seemed to him to be a cheap swindler, neither more nor less. But, swindler or not, if he could convince the court that he was the nephew of the old man who had died in Los Dipono so many years ago, he, and not Nick, would get the inheritance.

There were still several weeks before the hearing on the will, and Nick could do no more than hope that some way to prove his identity would turn up before that time. If it did not, then he would have to depend on convincing the court that he was the person named in the document.

Teddy told him about the latest arrival, "Break" O'Day, and of his "monk." At Roy's suggestion, he later repeated the story to his mother, so she would not worry any more about a savage animal being at large. Belle, when she heard of it, laughed aloud. But she admitted that the ape seemed anything but funny when she saw it in the woods.

Teddy and Roy were anxious to hear from Tod Jackson, to learn whether their trip to Big Bison Trail was going through all right. That evening Tod telephoned, saying that the company would leave in two or three days, and asking if the boys could go with them. Of course the answer was a decided yes. Tod also said that "Break" had found him and that he was going to make one of the party who were going to Big Bison. The boys were glad to hear that their eccentric acquaintance had at last gotten himself a job.

"Maybe we'll find his monkey for him," Roy said, as he and Teddy were preparing for bed that night "The ape seems to follow us around. If we ever do see him again, I think I'll take a chance and try to capture him. O'Day said he was tame."

"Tame or not, I fool around no apes," Teddy retorted. "Once was enough for me. Anyway, we have enough to think about, with Nick Looker and his money and our trip to Big Bison. Golly, Roy, I bet that'll be fun! Regular actors! A-hem! Out of my way, minion— I desire to retire!"

"Me, too—and I'm not a minion!" Roy grinned. "Me, I am a man of the films. Oh, yaass, I had a very hard day at the studio—a very hard day! Call me early, Francois. My press agent comes at eleven. Pass me those pink pajamas!"

CHAPTER XIII

THE LAWYER

On the day that Tod Jackson and the others were to start for Big Bison Trail there came an unexpected order for a large shipment of cattle to be sent from Eagles. This meant that all the X Bar X hands would be needed, and so Roy and Teddy were unable to accompany the moving picture company. But the delay was only temporary, and the two brothers arranged to meet Tod a few days later on the Trail. Tod had counted somewhat on the knowledge of Teddy and Roy to aid them in finding the Trail, but when the actor found he would have to start without them he made a map of the country, under the direction of Mr. Manley. With this in his possession as a guide, he set out for Big Bison Trail. The supplies were loaded into a car which was to follow Tod's auto, with Barton O'Day at the wheel.

The business of preparing the cattle for shipment took all of the boys' attention, and for three days they had little time to think of moving pictures. The firm that had given the order was most particular, and Mr. Manley told his sons that it was important they get the best cattle.

"Be sure every cow is O. K.," he cautioned. "Make two inspections. Nick, you see that none of 'em's underweight."

In the rush of rounding up the required number of cattle, Nick almost forgot that there was such a thing as an inheritance waiting for him. Nick was a puncher, body and soul, and when the range called everything else waited. At present it was his business to attend to the Durhams. If other things came up—well, he would see to them later. But just now that shipment had to be gotten off.

Nat Raymond was detailed to see that all strangers kept away from the cows while they were being "cut out." Teddy recalled Nat's ride after a phantom Denver Smith the day of the picnic, and wondered if any more alarms would be sounded. But Nat had evidently recovered from his suspicions, for the driving of the cattle to the freight station went off without a hitch.

"Though I did see two men riding somewhere in back of us," Nat declared later, in an uncertain tone of voice. "Course I can't tell who they were—"

"Maybe they were collection agents," Roy chuckled. "All paid up on your piano, Nat?"

"Huh—piano? What— Oh, that's meant to be a joke. Pardon me—I didn't see it. You ought to mark 'em, Roy. Honestly, there were two bozos behind us all the way in. One of 'em sure looked like the waddie I chased that day I met you an' Teddy and the girls by the river —you'd been fishin' or somethin'.''

"I remember," Roy said grimly. "Something else happened that day—but it's since been explained." He saw Nat looking at him queerly, and he made haste to ask:

"Nick ride in yet?"

Nat and Roy were standing in the ranch yard. The cattle had been taken to the station and things had once more settled down to dull routine.

"Not yet. Maybe he stopped off to see someone at Eagles. These last few days, when we were so busy, Nick was just like he used to be —you know, I mean singin' to himself an' everything. Before that he'd march around here as though somethin' was bitin' him. An' then as soon as he gets the cows off his hands he pulls a long face, an' now he's mournful again. What's the matter, anyhow?''

"Oh, Nick is funny that way," Roy answered carelessly. "Temperament, I guess. I'm going in an' wash up. That ride was some dusty. Say, if you see Nick tell him to wait for me, will you? Want to ask him something."

Nat nodded, and Roy turned away. Teddy was in his room trying to remove some of the dust that had accumulated on him from riding behind the cows, and Roy told him of Nat's two strangers.

"Aw, he's always seeing something mysterious," Teddy laughed. "Probably they were punchers from Pete Ball's ranch. We can't be keeping track of every rider that we see."

But they were not from the 8 X 8, as the boys found out when Nick arrived. As soon as Teddy saw the cowboy he knew that something was up. Nick tethered his pony to the hitching rail and walked slowly toward the bunkhouse. Teddy hailed him. He turned, and Teddy and Roy moved over to him.

"That's one job over," Roy declared, glancing at Nick keenly.

"Yea. Wish we had more of 'em."

"Well, we all do, I guess," Teddy laughed. "Stop off to grab a bite to eat, Nick?"

"Nope. Been talkin' to a feller."

"Uh-huh? Golly, it's hot. Probably rain before night."

"Been talkin' to a feller," Nick repeated. "A lawyer feller."

"You have?" Roy exclaimed. "What did he want?"

"Let's walk over this way," Nick said. When they were out of earshot of the bunkhouse he glanced around him.

"It was about that money," Nick said slowly.

Neither Teddy nor Roy spoke, deciding it was best to let Nick tell it his own way.

"This lawyer feller said he could get my inheritance for me."

Silence. Then Nick continued.

"He wanted ten per cent of what he gets. He followed us all the way to Eagles—him an' another guy."

"Nat wasn't so far wrong," Roy thought. Then, aloud, "What else did he say? We don't want to butt in, Nick, and if you'd rather—"

"You could never butt in," Nick said simply. "We're friends. Well, he said lots more. Said he heard tell that another feller was after the jack, too, an' I'd better step lively or he'd get it."

"Just how did he mean that, Nick?" Teddy asked deliberately.

"Yea, I know what yo're thinkin' of. If I didn't hire him he'd go to this other waddy— that's it, ain't it? Well, I kind of suspected that, so I told him I'd let him know. Blame that money, anyhow! It's got me so I don't sleep nights! Drivin' them cattle was the first real fun I've had in a long time, an' it's goin' some when yore job gets to be fun. But that's a fact. I stopped thinkin' about the inheritance for three whole days. Now it bobs up again. I want that money, or else I'd—"

"Certainly you want the money!" Teddy said quickly. "It's yours, and you ought to have it. Say, I'd like to talk to this lawyer."

"He's comin' over to see me to-morrow," Nick declared morosely. "Seems like you can't do nothin' in this country without the whole world knowin' about it.'' He shrugged his shoulders. ''Well, maybe it'll come out all right. That lawyer's name is—let's see now— I got it here some place—'' he searched his pockets, and brought forth a card. ''Jason Pettit, Attorney at Law,'' he read. ''Means a lawyer, I guess. Here—keep it. I'll lose it, sure.''

Roy smiled and took the card. ''We'll be here when he comes,'' he promised. ''I'd like to see what sort of a fellow Mr. Pettit is. Now forget about it for a while, Nick. Teddy, we'll wait until to-morrow before we start for Big Bison Trail. It'll take Tod and his bunch that long to get settled. We can leave to-morrow afternoon and, with luck, make the Trail by the next day.''

''With luck,'' Teddy repeated. ''That's some ride. But I'd like to hang around here for a while. Even if we are late for the scenes, we can't help it. Tod will understand.''

Teddy and Roy told their father of the lawyer. The ranch owner declared he would not trust a lawyer any further than he could see him—and Mrs. Manley, who overheard this, smiled and added:

''Some lawyers. Don't you remember when you wanted Roy to be a lawyer?''

Mr. Manley grinned. That had been in the days when he and Mrs. Manley were building air castles. Some of them had come true—and the others had turned into safe, comfortable houses with shining roofs. Too many castles never make a home—there must always be the low buildings.

Of course the boys knew nothing of their parents' thoughts, and if they had, Roy would probably have demanded more details until his father would laughingly have told him he'd write him a letter.

Teddy had already formed a picture of Jason Pettit in his mind; an image of a short, dark man with a mustache. Much to his surprise Pettit proved to be quite the opposite. He was tall and fair haired. He had no mustache, but Teddy thought his long upper lip might be improved by the addition of one. The man's eyes were small and set rather close together. But his smile was disarmingly frank.

He had gotten some one from the town to drive him over, and when he alighted from the car he saw Nick, Teddy, and Roy waiting for him near the ranch house. He held out his hand and walked forward.

"How are you, Mr. Looker?" he asked pleasantly. "I'm afraid I haven't met these gentlemen as yet."

"Teddy and Roy Manley," Nick said simply. "Their father owns this place."

Mr. Pettit looked about him with an air of eagerness which he immediately dissembled into a smile.

"Charming, charming," he murmured. "The real West. Well, Mr. Looker, if we might go some place and talk—"

"This is good enough for me," Nick said shortly. "Teddy and Roy know all about it. I told 'em."

"Indeed?" Pettit replied politely, but a queer look came into his eyes.

CHAPTER XIV

OFF TO BISON TRAIL

THERE was a short pause after Pettit's exclamation, but as no one else spoke he finally said:

"Then there's no objection to my speaking my mind, I presume. Now my idea is this."

Again there came a pause.

"It is sometimes very difficult to prove identity," Pettit went on. "Especially in cases of this sort, when one man's word is as good as another's. I suppose you realize that?"

Nick Looker nodded sadly. Teddy and Roy made no sign. The lawyer proceeded:

"Of course our idea would be to establish to the court's satisfaction that you are the Nicholas Looker named in the will. Now—"

"Say," Nick interrupted plaintively, "if it ain't premature or nothin', just how in thunder did you find out all this? Don't suppose you know where that quirt is that I lost last summer, do yuh?"

Pettit smiled blandly and shrugged his shoulders.

"The records of the court are available to
117

court officers," he declared smoothly. "Let us say that I happened to hear of your good fortune and determined to aid you. At all events, I know the facts concerning your inheritance. That shall be our starting point. Now to business. If I succeed in placing in your hands the six thousand dollars left you by your uncle, am I assured of a commission—let us say of ten per cent?"

Nick looked at Teddy and Roy.

"That seems fair," Roy said slowly. "If business is usually done in that way. Of course I don't know much about the practice of lawyers."

"I assure you it is," Pettit said dryly. "What do you say, Mr. Looker?" He turned away from Roy, a bit too obviously. Roy's eyes narrowed.

"Well, six thousand bucks is a lot of money," Nick declared in a low tone. "I'd sure like to cash in on it. May I ask how yo're gonna get it for me?"

"If it's all the same to you, I'd rather not say," Pettit answered. Then he winked. "What you don't know won't hurt you."

"Sometimes," Teddy broke in. "Pettit, just how are you going about this thing?" he suddenly asked, and sharply.

Pettit gazed at the boy keenly, then allowed his eyes to travel the length of Teddy's figure.

"Really," he murmured, "my business is with Mr. Looker. I fail to see—"

"That's all right," Nick snapped out. "Yore business is with them, too. Go ahead —spill it! I'm kinda curious myself now."

Pettit shrugged his shoulders again.

"If you insist, then I suppose I must tell you," he grumbled. "The trouble is, Mr. Looker, that you have no birth certificate. I propose to remedy that defect."

"Huh? I don't get yuh. Say it slow, will yuh?"

"I said I intend to see that when the court opens on your case that it has before it a birth certificate, properly sworn to, that you, and none other, are the man named in the will. This will be accomplished through a friend of mine who has a certain facility with the—er— pen. I trust your question is answered?"

"It is," Nick said grimly. He yawned and stretched. "Well, I got to be goin'. Teddy, take this letter to your dad, will you? Got it while I was at Eagles."

"But here!" Pettit interrupted, in a star- tled voice. "What's the matter? Aren't you in on this with me?"

Nick turned and looked the lawyer full in the face.

"Unless I'm mistaken," he murmured softly, "you said you'd get a certificate made for me?"

"Why, yes, that's the general idea. But you'll have nothing to do with that. All you do is to collect the money."

"So that's all, is it?" Nick repeated. He appeared to be thinking deeply. It was some moments before he spoke. "I used to know a feller," he continued in a musing tone, "who done a lot of fishin'. But he never caught nothin'. Once a man came along an' told him if he put a load of dynamite in the lake an' set it off he'd have all the fish he needed. So this feller done it. Well, sir, he put too much dynamite there—an' he stood too close. Moral: the worse you want a thing, the more careful you want to be how you get it. That mean anything to you?" He eyed Pettit closely.

"I fail to see—" the lawyer began, when Nick stepped forward.

"Listen," he said fiercely. "I want that money, an' I want it bad. But I ain't forgin' no certificates to get it! If I can't get it straight, she lays there an' rots! Get me? Now vamose before I turn the hose on yuh!"

For a moment Pettit stood there, his mouth partly open, a startled look in his eyes. Then he laughed shortly.

"Very well," he said bitterly. "The yokel has spoken. I bid you adieu. And you can kiss that money good-bye, too. You'll never see it, you jackanapes!"

"What's that you called me?" Nick demanded, an ominous gleam in his eyes. Teddy put a firm hand on his arm.

"Let him go, Nick," the boy advised. "He isn't worth it. What's the use of cluttering up the landscape?"

"That's right," Nick agreed, relaxing. He stood quietly while the lawyer walked over to the car and got in. But as the auto pulled out of the yard the cowboy snapped his fingers smartly.

"Shucks," he grumbled in a disgusted voice. "I could have taken one crack at him, for luck. The blamed ole polecat! Suggestin' that I go in on a dirty scheme like that! Suppose they found out the certificate was faked?"

"I had that very thought in mind," Roy confessed. "His story sounded fishy to me. Well, he's gone now, and I guess you told him where you stood. I reckon he'll team up with that other Nick Looker now."

"Let him," Nick grunted. "Those two 'ud make a fine pair. But I'll have no crooked work in mine. The money ain't worth that much."

The most obvious result of the lawyer's visit was to make Nick more morose and dissatisfied with life. The less obvious result, but for that reason probably the most important, was to bring to Nick's mind the fact that money as such had peculiar drawing powers. Constantly there was forced into his consciousness the thought of that six thousand dollars, as a desperately thirsty man looks at a glass of sea-water before him. If there were only some way of getting it, some way that did not involve the plain forgery Pettit had suggested! But forgery was forgery, and a crime. Money so obtained would be valueless.

"I ain't goin' to do nothin' dishonest," muttered Nick to himself, savagely. "I want to pay Ham back—got to—but it ain't goin' to be with boodle I don't get honestly, no sir!"

Soon after the lawyer left, Teddy and Roy prepared to make the trip to Big Bison Trail. On their saddles hung bags of provisions and blankets and, of course, their rifles. Flash and Star, the broncos, stood pawing the ground as the boys said their farewells. Belle was disappointed, and she made no bones about the fact.

"What do boys care about movies? Why can't I, and not you, be taking the trip to Big Bison Trail to be in the pictures?"

At least she had been in one, and perhaps, when the company returned, she would be used again. Teddy was instructed to drop veiled remarks in the hearing of Tod about the ability of his sister.

Nell and "Curley" waved good-bye. Mr. Manley called out: "Good luck!" Mrs. Manley stood on the porch, smiling.

At three in the afternoon the two riders left

the ranch yard. By four o'clock they were out
of sight of the X Bar X, and on the first leg
of their journey. Their way lay almost at
right angles to Rocky Run River, directly into
the mountains. For some distance the ground
was fairly level, but as the sun was setting they
came to their first steep ascent. The mountain
rose towering before them, the path they were
to take circling it like a girdle of brown autumn
leaves. The trail stood out plainly against the
green of the rest of the picture.

Teddy halted Flash and looked up at the
mountain.

"Calls for effort," he stated. "Effort calls
for energy. Energy calls for food. Let's eat!"

"A suggestion worthy of a poet," Roy commented. "As Robert Burns says—"

"Just as he says," Teddy interrupted. "I
believe you have the bacon on your horse.
May I help you?"

"You may not." Roy alighted, threw Star's
bridle over the low limb of a near-by tree
and removed the bags and his gun from his
saddle.

"You start the fire," Roy suggested. "I
shall attempt to prepare the edibles for internal consumption."

"I see you were impressed by Pettit," came
from Teddy. "You talk like him now."

"The lawyer?" Roy snorted disdainfully.
"He was a bag of wind—and a big bag at that.

If Nick falls for his line of gab he's simpler than I think he is.''

"That's right." Teddy loosened Flash's girth a trifle and sent the pony to join Star. "Wish Nick had come with us. That Pettit isn't finished yet—he'd never give up that easily. Wonder how he heard about the money —all the way from New York. And that other bird—the actor that Tod fired—how'd he ever get wind of it? By jimminy, Roy, I have an idea! I'll bet—"

"Not with me, you won't," Roy said decid-dedly. "I thought of that long ago. Pettit and that actor are together in this deal. Remember Nat Raymond said *two* men were following us to Eagles? The actor was the other, or I miss my guess. He'll show up later. Poor Nick! He's a popular guy right now! Wonder if he ever will get that six thousand!''

CHAPTER XV

IN THE QUICKSAND

THE little flame Teddy was nursing sprang into an active, eager fire, crackling joyfully. Two green sticks were implanted on each side of it, and the pan was suspended by the simple method of wedging it between the notched twigs. Into the pan was thrown sliced bacon—much of it. It sizzled resentfully, and the fragrant aroma swept in a delicious breath to the boys' nostrils.

"Bacon," Roy muttered, "is a gift to man often lightly passed over. Few appreciate its virtues. It solaces the weary, brings forgetfulness to the sick at heart, nourishes the hungry. It—"

"Turn it over," Teddy said laconically. "Burned bacon tastes rotten."

Roy subsided into silence, and stood, hands on hips, watching the flames lick the frying pan. Now and then a bit of grease would hop over the sides into the fire, causing the blaze to shoot a mischievous tongue toward the crisping bacon. This was the signal for frantic stirrings to prevent scorching.

When the meat was done, it was laid with great care on slices of bread and placed near the fire to keep warm, and baked beans took its place in the pan. Then the coffee, which had been set in its pot within the embers, was tested and pronounced perfect. The meal was ready. The banqueters sat down to their feast.

"This bacon," Roy said slowly, "is good."

"Uh!" grunted Teddy. With an effort he swallowed. "Yea," was his further contribution to the conversation, and he proceeded to the business at hand.

When supper was over, the boys debated the question of traveling on or spending the night where they were. Roy said that if they were going to make Big Bison Trail the next day, or even on the morning of the day following, it would be well to cover as much ground as possible before they camped.

"I don't like night riding, myself," he admitted. "But we can't very well get lost if we stick to that trail," and he pointed toward the mountain.

"You're the doctor," Teddy answered, and shrugged his shoulders. "As long as we're going, let's start before dark. Maybe we can cross Lonely River and camp on the other side of that."

Roy arose and began stowing away the supper things. The river Teddy mentioned was really little more than a creek, although in some spots it widened sufficiently to serve as an excuse for its name. It lay on the other side of the mountain.

With the camp things once more on the saddles, the boys went on.

Although these spring days were short, yet their twilight lasted some time, and the riders were well into the mountain before the first stars peeped through the sky. The slight breeze had died with the coming of night, and the only sounds to be heard were the soft thud of the ponies' feet on the ground. The conversation languished, then stopped altogether. There is something about night riding among the hills of the West that makes words seem insignificant, futile. It is better to let thought travel its own path, unimpeded by talk. At times like this, fancy roams freely, leaping from one topic to another, like a bird flitting back and forth in flight.

The trail wound its way about the mountain. At ten o'clock the boys felt the path dip, and within half an hour they came to the river. The spring rains had swelled it somewhat, and the opposite bank, looming dark and strange in the faint moonlight, was further away than they had expected.

"There's a ford a bit below," Roy said carelessly. "Want to try that or shall we cross here?"

"What's the use of going out of our way? I've gone over this before, and never had to look for a ford. Why—don't think it's deep, do you?"

"No; I know it's not. But the bottom isn't good. The sand is soft. Shouldn't want to get stuck."

"With these broncs? Say, Flash can pull out of anything. Of course I don't know about Star—"

"Don't worry about him," Roy answered shortly. "If Flash can do it, Star can."

Silently Teddy guided his horse to the edge.

"Take it, Flash," he said softly. "In you go!"

The pony hesitated for a moment, then, with a little whinny, he stepped forward. The next moment he was up to his neck in water.

"Come back!" Roy shouted frantically. "The bank has been washed out!"

"Think I don't know that?" Teddy yelled testily. "It's too late now! Up, Flash, up! Hold to it! Steady—"

The horse was struggling wildly. The drop had been so sudden he had not been prepared for it, and for a moment he lost his head. Roy, powerless to aid, watched with anxious eyes the desperate attempt of Flash to return.

"Let him have his head, Teddy!" Roy called. Then, as a sudden fear came to him, he unwound the rope which hung from his saddle.

If Flash should get caught in the treacherous bottom!

"Don't throw that!" Teddy yelled, for he saw his brother's purpose. "I'll make it! Over, Flash, over! Not back—forward! That's it!"

Giving up his intention to reach the shore he had just left, the pony faced the opposite bank and began swimming strongly. Roy breathed a sigh of relief as he saw this. Flash had recovered himself now, and was swimming calmly. He reached the middle of the stream, and turning his head Teddy called:

"We're O.K. now! See you on the other side!"

"Hope so," Roy breathed. "But I think I'll try that ford. No point to making Star use up his energy that way. We have plenty of ride ahead of us."

He did not start immediately, but waited until Teddy had almost reached the opposite bank. Then he raised his voice in a shout:

"I'm going downstream a way! You wait there, and I'll ride up. Hear me?"

"Yep! Go ahead and—Roy! Roy!"

The sudden cry caused Roy's heart to leap to his throat. It was desperate, intense—the call of a person in danger.

"What's the matter, Teddy?" he asked quickly. Then he peered across the water and saw the answer to his question. Flash had stopped swimming. His body was high out of water, but he was not moving, except for the frantic tossing of his head. Teddy sat as still as death in the saddle, one hand holding the reins in a grip of steel.

Then he called again—his voice sounding hoarse, fraught with disaster.

"Roy—the sand! It's got us! Come! I can't— Flash—"

Roy, his eyes wide with fright, saw something that he could never forget to his dying day. Slowly, so slowly that it was almost imperceptible, the water crept higher and higher toward Flash's back.

"Teddy! Hold on! I'm coming!"

Heedless of consequences, the boy literally threw Star into the water. Shouting and yelling like an insane person, Roy forced the bronco toward his brother and the horse that stood caught in the quicksand that was slowly sucking them to their death.

"The rope, Roy," Teddy called calmly, as though he had said, "My hat, Roy." Teddy knew their one chance lay in keeping cool and thinking things out. He was devoting all his attention to quieting Flash. Every movement of the poor beast was drawing him deeper down into the river. The water was up to his chest now. Soon, soon—

"Get off, Teddy!" Roy shouted. "Get off and swim!"

"Not yet. Flash is under me. We'll come out of this together."

Roy understood. Teddy, careless, happy-go-lucky Teddy, was staying with his horse. Roy took a deep breath, gauged the distance still remaining between him and his brother, loosened the rope, and threw.

CHAPTER XVI

A Lariat Rescue

The cast of the lariat was short. Roy's pony, obedient to a firm pull on his reins, was striving to keep his place in the water without getting too near Teddy. The plunging bronco's breath came in great gasps. Several times he whinnied reproachfully, but Roy held him sternly to the task.

As the rope lashed the water, Teddy turned his head hopefully. But it was far out of his reach.

"The next time, Roy," he said cheerfully, as though Roy, and not he, were in need of encouragement. "We're not sinking so fast now. Maybe we've struck hard sand. Steady, Flash—"

Roy drew in the lariat quickly. Star was swimming in circles now, and Roy could feel the pony's sides expand and contract with the agony of effort. He dared not send him closer to Teddy, for fear he, too, would be seized by the treacherous quicksand.

"All right, Teddy old boy!" Roy called. "This time, now—this is the one!"

Again the lariat uncurled out over the blue-black water. A little spatter of drops fell from it as it flew through the air. A moment of intense suspense, when the rope seemed to hang in the air—then it settled, full over the boy and horse.

"Got it!" Teddy yelled wildly, his desperately enforced calmness deserting him. "Take us out, Roy, take us out—" There was fear in his voice, fear for the first time. The water was licking greedily at the pony's chin.

"Get it under his chest! Under his chest and around back of the saddle! All right? Is it fixed? Star can't stay here much longer!"

"Wait—just a minute! She's on! To the shore, quick! I'm—" The rest of the sentence was lost. Teddy had thrown himself from the horse and was making for the bank ahead of him.

Roy urged Star to the edge of the stream. For a moment he had a sudden fear that the horse would not be able to climb the enbankment, that he would have to swim further downstream. The rope was not long enough for that. If Star was too weak to get a foothold on the side, Roy would have to relinquish the rope and watch it go floating out of reach, the other end about Flash, the pony waiting patiently for the lariat to tighten and pull him clear, and instead to watch him sink deeper, his nose held pitifully above the dark waters.

"We've got to make it, Star! Got to!"

They came to the shore. Roy felt the pony's forefeet touch upon earth. With his knees griping the horse's sides, with every atom of his desire concentrated on getting the bronco up, as though he could force him on with his will, Roy lifted Star out of the water—*lifted* him, and stood, trembling violently, on the bank, the rope still in his hand.

He heard Teddy call from the opposite bank, but could not make out the words. There seemed to be a ringing in his ears, as though a thousand bells were clanging. But his work was before him.

"Get along, Star! Good ole hoss! Now!" The rope tightened. Star's muscles hardened into knots of steel. He strained forward.

From the middle of Lonely River came a scream of agony as the rope bit into Flash's chest. Gritting his teeth Roy forced his pony on.

"This is for Teddy, old horse," he muttered. "We want to get his Flash for him. Go ahead!" he yelled suddenly, savagely.

Star quivered under the terrific effort. Another scream sounded, a call, a frantic plea to cool the fire that was scorching the pony's flesh. Roy closed his eyes. He brought his heels into Star's belly with a vicious dig. The lariat tightened again, and vibrated like a living thing.

"On, Star, on! Forget those screams! On!"

Then, as an octopus who has lost the fight releases his prey, the sand gave up its victim. The rope slackened. Then it twisted and turned, almost joyfully, as though it were delivered from captivity. On the far end, instead of a dead weight there was a living, breathing, swimming horse.

"Teddy! Teddy! We got him! He's out! Yay, Teddy! He's almost to the bank! We can pull him up there, can't we, old boy? Hard! Up, now!"

Flash, with the lariat still about him, dripping water—and blood—stood on the bank, shivering, trembling, but safe.

Roy slid from his pony, struck the ground, and pitched forward on his face. His legs seemed turned to straw. But he was up again in a moment and alongside Flash, soothing him, removing the rope with hands as gentle as those of a woman. Even in that semi-blackness he could see the huge welt about the horse's chest where the lariat had cut in, bringing those horrible screams.

It was over now. Roy put his cupped hands to his lips.

"Teddy! Hear me? Teddy!"

Clearly the answer came ringing back:

"He's all right!"

"Yo-o-o! How's Flash?"

Roy walked toward the bank again, and, peering across, made out his brother's figure on the opposite side.

"I'll take the two horses down to the ford. Half a mile below here. You're not hurt?"

"Don't worry about me, Roy. Wet, that's all. If I had come ashore any sooner Flash would have tried to get out to follow me, and he would have mired himself deeper. I can't yell any more—I'm hoarse now. Head for that ford."

His voice ceased, and Roy saw the figure step back and out of sight. Roy returned to the ponies. Speaking soothingly to Flash, he led them both downstream, himself walking ahead.

Twenty minutes later he came to the spot where the river ran almost as shallow as a brook, and Roy once more remounted Star. He urged him forward fearlessly. The bottom of the river gleamed up at him, pebble white. No dark sand here. In a moment he was across. He sat down on a log by the side of the stream to wait for Teddy.

When he came, Roy saw on his left check a dark, sullen streak with smeared edges.

"Rope caught me," Teddy said simply. "Burned me. Let's see Flash now. Flash!"

He reached out and seized the horse's head with both hands, pulling the eyes down to a level with his own. The pony, who had been breathing excitedly, whinnied and stood perfectly still, calm and cool. His breath came smoothly. The quivering of his haunches stopped.

Roy sat quiet, watching the strange spectacle of the horse and boy in the faint light. Some-how, his brother seemed like another person, a stranger he had come upon in the forest. Then Teddy spoke:

"Got you too, old boy. Let's see. No won-der you screamed! That'll soon be better. Here!"

Taking out his handkerchief, Teddy soaked it in the stream and sponged the pony's chest. A shudder passed over the animal's body, as a man from whose flesh a cauterizing iron has been taken trembles with relief, at the blessed coolness.

Roy arose and came toward Teddy. He placed his hands on his brother's shoulders and looked at his face.

"That's bad, Teddy," he said sharply. "It's a real cut. Forget Flash for a minute. He's all right now. Come over here."

He led his brother to the stream. There he washed and cleansed the wound and bound it up with a clean dry handkerchief.

"Roy," Teddy said presently, "I'm not go-ing to spill a lot of fireworks. I want to say only one thing. Thanks for saving my horse."

"Sure, Teddy," Roy replied, and grinned. "You'd do the same for me. Let's get the leather off the broncs. Here's where we camp."

Teddy nodded. He returned to Flash and gently removed the saddle. Then he led the horse back a way, to where there was grazing, and turned him loose. He knew Flash would not wander, and he wanted the horse to have freedom of motion, so that he would not be too stiff in the morning.

Once more a campfire was built, and Teddy dried himself. Not a thing had been lost in the river. The rifles were wet, but a judicious polishing with an oiled handkerchief put them in shape again. The boys did this before they turned in. Naturally the blankets were sodden, but the night was warm, and neither suffered from exposure. The fire died down. The river, friendly now, murmured as it crept over the stony bottom. A light breeze came up. The boys slept.

They awoke to a dull, cloudy morning. Teddy was the first one to rouse up and he stretched prodigiously, leaned over, and kicked Roy.

"Huh!" Roy muttered, and opened eyes heavy with slumber. He saw the face of his brother grinning at him. "Some sleep! I feel like—Oh, my back!" He reached underneath him and with an impatient jerk brought forth a small bent stick. "That thing's been bothering me all night. Dreamed a cannibal was trying to puncture me with a spear."

He lay still for a moment, gazing at the sky.

"Rain, I guess," he murmured. "Think so?"

No answer came. Teddy had left, and was leading Flash up to Roy.

"Say good-morning, bronc," Teddy said. "Here's your rescuer. He's the one who gave you that brand on your chest and this one on my face, but we'll forgive him for that; hey, ole hoss?"

"Sorry," Roy replied, sitting up. "Couldn't be helped, Teddy. Does it hurt now?"

"Certainly not, you six-toed frog," Teddy laughed. "And what if it does? You know I was only kidding." He leaned with his knees upon his brother's shoulders, and pulled Flash's head down. "Kiss him, bronc," he ordered "Give him a good, big smack."

"He'll give me no good, big smack," Roy yelled, leaping to his feet. "What do you think I am? Let him alone now and help with breakfast. Snakes, I'm starved! Bring in that roast turkey."

The effect of the night's adventure wore off with the internal application of bacon and coffee. The wound on Flash's chest was examined, and although it was terribly raw and sore, yet the pony had not stiffened up, and took his saddle without a murmur. Teddy gazed at the river toward the spot where the quicksand had laid its tentacles about his pony's feet. The stream flowed placidly by, to all appearances as innocent as any lake.

"Liar," Teddy muttered, and picking up a stone, he scaled it far up the river. "Your evil heart is hidden beneath a smiling face. You are a wolf in sheep's clothing. You are a monster, luring—oh, applesauce! You give me a pain in the neck!"

The provisions and camp supplies were collected and fastened tightly to the saddles. Then the boys mounted, to start the last leg of their journey to Big Bison Trail.

CHAPTER XVII

The Rearing Bronco

A cloudy sky changed to a perfect blue as the day wore on, and Big Bison Trail was reached late that afternoon. The boys came upon it as they topped a small rise, and saw it before them in all the glory of the lowered sun. To the right and left huge mountains of reddish stone raised their impersonal heads. Between them lay the Trail.

It took its name from happenings now long past. On this grassy floor thousands—even hundreds of thousands—of bisons had plodded their stolid ways toward newer feeding grounds or toward the corrals of the Indians, driven by a few feathered braves. The Trail was deep and broad. Its length was dotted with water holes, like the imprints of smudgy fingers in the virgin green of the grass. Some freak of nature had wiped it clean of trees and brush, leaving it open to the sun, frank, unashamed. As far as the eye could reach, the verdant carpet was unrolled between the mountains, for, with the passing of the bison, grass grew over the trail.

Roy sat silently in the saddle, his eyes drinking in the wonderful sight. Even Teddy was at a loss for words. It all seemed too great, too stupendous, as though they had suddenly come upon a field of emeralds.

Then Teddy clucked to his bronco, and the two boys came into the grassy plain.

"I wonder," Teddy said, "where Tod and the others are."

Roy shrugged his shoulders. He was still under the spell of nature, and Teddy looked over at him and grinned. "This is the forest primeval," he muttered. "The murmuring pines and the hemlocks—hey, Roy!"

"What?" Roy turned startled eyes on his brother.

"Nothing! Didn't want you to go to sleep, that was all. As I remarked before, when so rudely interrupted by your flow of language, I wonder where Tod Jackson is?"

"I wonder. That what I'm supposed to say? Well, they can't be far. I suppose they'd wait at, or near, the entrance. We'll ride on a bit and see if we can find them."

They did find them shortly, camped like Persian kings close to the side of the mountain. Marvel Films had sent three more men out to help Tod, and the whole group was seated in one of the tents eating dinner—or supper, in that country—when the boys rode up. Teddy nudged Roy as he saw the three tents, the shel-

ter for the autos, the elaborate cooking arrangements.

"Everything but a swimming pool," he
chuckled. "They sure did it up brown."

When Tod saw his two friends he was unaf-
fectedly delighted. He introduced them to the
new members of the cast, and bade them sit
down to a regular meal.

"What kind of ice-cream?" he asked.

The boys smiled.

"Huckleberry," Roy laughed.

"Break" O'Day was very much in evidence,
and he inquired eagerly if the boys had seen his
baboon. When they told him they had not, he
seemed sorrowful for a moment, then brightened.

"We'll find him some day," he declared.
"Stands to reason an animal can't mislay himself like that. An' say, I got me a peach of a
job! Tell 'em Tod."

"Comedian," Tod explained. "He's good,
too."

"Betcha," Break said proudly. "Had a
lot of footage already. Maybe I'll star
soon." He winked at Teddy. "Seems like
Sam here—" he motioned to the director—
"just wants me to be natural. That's the
easiest thing I do. What do you think of our
quarters?"

"Where's the library?" Teddy asked.
"Guess you're not so very high-hat. Boy, I'd

like to live here myself! Snappy, I call it. When do we start work, Tod?"

The screen star said he hoped things would be all set for the morrow. They had not done much that day, as the sun was not right—the light was too poor. There were some close-ups to be taken of Miss Harper, and Sam wanted her "shot" while on a horse.

After an excellent meal the two boys wandered out of the mess tent, and Sam continued his conversation in the open air.

"Miss Harper can't ride very well," he explained, "an' I don't want no accidents. So I had a pony that was guaranteed to be safe brought over for her." He motioned toward the rear of the camp. "Got him tied up there. We want to get that scene to-morrow early, then you two come in. Teddy, you're booked up for some fast riding."

"Suits me," Teddy nodded. "I'll do the best I can. Maybe Roy—"

"Maybe Roy nothing," interrupted his brother. "You're a better rider than I am, and you know it, Teddy Manley. What's the scene, Sam?"

"Well, Miss Harper is supposed to be riding this pony I spoke of, and he runs away with her. We can fake that part of it, but the rescue has to be real. And there, my boy, is where you come in."

"Who, me?" Teddy asked in surprise. "I

thought Tod would do that. He's the hero, isn't he?"

"Well, officially he *does* do it," Sam replied. "But we want you to double for him. Of course if you object—"

"What? Object? I should say not! Glad of the chance. Do I look enough like Tod to fool the camera?"

"When the camera wants to be fooled it's the easiest thing in the world to trick it. You'll do nicely. To-morrow morning, then."

Later the boys were shown their cots. Miss Harper and Miss De Lisle of course had one of the tents to themselves, and the men were divided between the other two. There was no crowding, and all were comfortable. There was a smaller shelter in the rear for the cook and his helper, and then the lean-to for the cars. All in all, it was a complete camp.

When Teddy complimented Tod on the perfection of the arrangements, the actor said that since they could not tell just how long they would have to remain, he thought it best to make themselves comfortable.

"This business waits on the weather," he told the boys. "If a series of bad days come, we have to stop work and wait until they're over. So far we've been pretty lucky. Thought we were in for a storm this morning, but she blew over. Hope it's clear to-morrow."

"Have you seen any more of that actor you

discharged?'' Roy asked. ''He didn't try to make trouble?''

''None that I've heard of. Saw him in Eagles the day we left, but he didn't say a word. Guess he's finished. He had a fine nerve to use us to come out here to impersonate some one else! If I had known that in the beginning, I'd never have taken him on. But we were hard up for some one, and he happened to fit in.''

''Say, Tod,'' Teddy broke in, ''you didn't see a tall, blond man around town—a man with eyes set close together?''

Tod Jackson thought for a moment.

''Yes, now that you mention it, I did. He was with this fake Nick Looker. Why?''

''He was with him!'' Roy repeated. ''We were right, Teddy! Just what you suggested!''

They told Tod of Pettit's visit and of his proposal to secure a forged birth certificate for Nick. Tod nodded understandingly.

''Heard of that game before,'' he said briefly. ''This Pettit is a good man to steer clear of. I certainly hope your Nick Looker gets his money. I'd rather see no one get it than have that bird we so kindly brought with us stick his hands into it. When we finish here, we'll see what we can do to help your man. If that would-be actor tries to put anything over on the court we may be able to spike his guns.''

After a few more minutes conversation Roy and Teddy determined to seek their bunks.

They told Tod of their experience with the quicksand, and he expressed his concern over Teddy's narrow escape.

"Be a shame to lose that splendid animal of yours," he commented. "He certainly is a wonder. Almost looks as though he could speak. Well, see you in the morning, boys. Happy dreams!"

The cots were soft and grateful to the tired bodies of the two riders. They awoke early, however, much refreshed and ready for breakfast. This meal assumed almost the dignity of a function. The company sat down to a long table and were served by the cook's helper, who carried the food in from the cooking tent on a large tray. It seemed that these people were used to taking their work in easy stages, first making sure that their bodily wants were taken care of. Teddy contrasted this camp with some of those he had spent nights in—where a blanket, a fire, and a rifle were the only comforts.

When the last cup of coffee was finished and the last bit of toast nibbled, the company arose from the table.

"Want that riding scene this morning, Sam?" Tod asked, as he walked out into the sunshine. "It's a corking day."

"If I can get it. Miss Harper, feel equal to a little rough work?"

"And it will be rough—on me," Miss Harper answered, smiling. "I haven't ridden for so long I'm almost afraid to try a horse again."

"Not this horse," Sam declared. "We got him special for you. He wouldn't bolt if he saw a train coming at him. Stay here, and I'll bring him over. Tod, you get your pony, will you?"

"Thought Tod and the others came in cars," Teddy said in an aside to Roy. "How'd the horses get here?"

"Must have been brought over later," his brother answered. "Golly, what a bronc!"

Sam had returned, leading a sorry looking specimen of the horse tribe. His skin was good and he was not so awfully bony, but there was a certain dejected appearance about him that was pathetic.

"Here's the charger," Sam chuckled. "Think you can sit on him for a few minutes, Miss Harper?"

"I'll have to, I suppose," and the girl smiled nervously. "You're sure he won't run away or anything?"

"Not this bird." Sam rubbed the pony's nose. The horse looked at him reproachfully, as much as to say: "Why can't you let me alone? All I want is rest!"

Now Tod Jackson rode forward on a bronco that stepped high and held his head proudly.

"There's a horse," Teddy breathed. "What a difference between the two!"

"Yes—and maybe there's a difference you

didn't notice," Roy said quietly. "That old plug there isn't safe. See his eyes? He looks sleepy enough; but when that kind wakes up, there's fireworks! I will admit that it takes a great deal to wake them up—usually nothing short of an earthquake will do it. I wonder if we ought to—"

"And get laughed at?" Teddy interrupted, realizing what his brother was going to suggest. "Why, if we told them that ole Spindle-shanks was dangerous they'd think we were crazy. Tell you—we'll stand by, on Flash and Star, in case anything turns up. Tod is a fair enough rider, I guess, but—"

He did not finish, though Roy knew what he meant. The way Tod Jackson sat in the saddle was an indication that he had not spent much time on the back of a horse. His body was held too stiffly and his legs failed to grip the pony's sides with the assurance that is the mark of an expert rider.

Roy and Teddy watched with interest the setting up of the cameras. This scene was going to be taken without rehearsal, and to make sure that one perfect picture would be made of it, so that it would not have to be shot again, two cameras were being used.

"Are we about ready, Lem?" Tod called to the camera man.

"Just about, Mr. Jackson. All right. We can start now."

"Miss Harper," the director called. "I'm going to ask you to use a little of that nerve for which you are justly famous." He grinned, and Miss Harper dropped a curtsey in mock appreciation. "You know we've got to fake a runaway. Well, I want to rear that hatrack of yours."

"You mean—"

"Now don't get scared. All I want is just one little shot of you on the horse, and the horse up on his hind legs. All you have to do is pull up on the reins, and hang on for a second. Then we'll cut, and fake the rest. Think you can do it?"

Miss Harper looked at the pony. Then she smiled, a trifle nervously, and threw up one hand in a dramatic gesture.

"I die for my art! Lead me to the ferocious beast! Come what may, I will never break faith with my public!"

"Atta baby," Sam said, grinning. "Up you go, Miss Harper. Get set now, boys—we don't want to take this again. You come in from left, Miss Harper. When you get here—" he marked the ground with his heel—"you pull him up. He'll take it all right. The man I got him from said he was well trained. All right. Let's start."

Quietly Teddy and Roy slipped to the rear and hurried toward Flash and Star. Their horses had already been saddled, probably by

one of the helpers, who thought they belonged
to the company. The boys mounted.

They walked their horses to a spot from which
they could see the action of the picture. The
cameras were ready to start grinding. Miss
Harper sat on the pony, a smile on her lips, but
the boys could plainly see the paleness of her
face.

"She's a game kid," Roy declared admiringly. "Scared to death, but she's going
through with it. See how her hand trembles!"

"Too bad they couldn't get some one else,"
Teddy said sympathetically. "But I suppose
it's all in the game. Reckon they're starting
now."

The voice of Sam, strident, imperious, broke
the silence.

"Action! Camera! Walk him on now, Miss
Harper. That's it. Not too fast! Remember
where I made that mark. When you get there,
pull him up hard. That's fine. Make believe
you're on a stroll with your pet horse or something. Good! Take all the footage you want.
Now stop, and gaze into the distance toward the
mountains. We'll take a long shot of them
later. All right. Now forward. Remember
that mark. Follow her, boys. Be sure she's in
focus all the time. Get set, Miss Harper! The
mark's just ahead of you! Got her all in, boys?
A little more, Miss Harper. Now! Pull him

up! Pull him up! Harder! Monkeys, he's stubborn! Yank him!''

The girl, white-faced and trembling, was jerking frantically on the reins. For a moment it looked as though the horse were sound asleep on his feet. He seemed scarcely to breathe. Then, with the suddenness of a coiled spring, the pony reared. His head snapped back. The martingale, which Tod had insisted be put on the pony to prevent just this, quickly parted.

"Hit him with the crop!" Teddy yelled. "Bring him down! Snakes, he'll kill her!"

Whether Miss Harper heard the advice or not, no one could tell. Perhaps she was too frightened to take advantage of it. The horse, snorting in rage, again tossed his head back. His hard skull caught Miss Harper full on the forehead. With a moan she crumpled forward, her nerveless hands releasing the reins, her body slumped over the saddle. The horse, realizing he was free, leaped high, and, taking the bit between his teeth, plunged forward. The body of the actress, limp on the pony's back her feet tangled in the stirrups, swayed from side to side!

CHAPTER XVIII

JUST IN TIME

YELLING! Cries of "Get her! Get her!" An aimless rushing about.

Tod, in his excitement, was holding the reins of his pony so tightly that the beast, instead of following the runaway, was backing.

"Come out of it, you!" Tod shouted. Slap! His riding crop lashed the pony's sides. But the horse was not the type that responds to this sort of treatment. Then Tod looked up and saw ahead of him two figures who, bent low over their mounts, were flying across the plain.

"Save her, boys—for heaven's sake, save her! She's—"

Neither Teddy nor Roy heard the frantic appeal. They were riding silently, swiftly. By some miracle the girl remained in the saddle, probably because her hands were unconsciously gripping the pommel. But both Teddy and Roy knew that at any moment her grasp might be dislodged, and down to the ground she would pitch, one foot caught in the stirrup, her face near those flying feet.

153

"Thank goodness he's a plug," Roy thought. "He can't last much longer."

They were overtaking the runaway, but slowly. Rage seemed to lend wings to the horse ahead. His neck stretched forward, his feet beating a dull tattoo, he surged onward. Gradually, however, he appeared to falter.

"Now, Teddy!" Roy yelled, and let Star have his head. Closer and closer the two riders came to the unconscious girl, until they could see her hunched shoulders, her white face, a dark blotch of blood on her forehead where the pony's head had struck her.

"She's falling!" The cry burst from Teddy's lips, and fiercely he spurred Flash. "We've got to—"

Then, suddenly, it was over. The horse with the girl on his back weakened and stumbled. In an instant the two riders were at his side.

"Left!" Teddy yelled. Roy swerved, and came up on the left. Teddy was opposite him.

Almost as though it had been rehearsed many times, the boys leaned out. An arm of each seized the girl. They lifted. Spindle-shanks pitched forward, fell heavily. But the girl was not under him. She was being carried along by Roy and Teddy.

"He's done," Teddy said, looking back at the fallen horse.

"Miss Harper! Here! Wake up! Teddy, slide off there! Lift her down!"

Teddy obeyed promptly. Flash stood quietly as the boy slid to the ground and relieved Roy of his burden. Gently he laid the girl on the sod.

"She got a terrific sock," Teddy remarked briefly. "If we had some water we could bathe her head. Jimminy, it's hot!"

"A fine time to think about the heat!" Roy exclaimed. "Can't you see she might be dead? That ride—"

"Not—not dead yet," said a tiny voice, and Miss Harper opened her eyes and looked about her. "I—I guess I'm supposed to say 'Where am I?' But I know. Heavens, my head aches!"

"Now, now just take it easy," Roy soothed. He shifted from one foot to the other awkwardly. Maidens in distress had not been a common experience in his life. "You'll be all right soon, Miss Harper. You were hit on the head."

"There's no doubt of that," Miss Harper murmured. Making an effort, she sat up. "I'm afraid I'm not being very grateful to my rescuers," and she smiled weakly. "But I feel so funny—"

"Sure! I know!" Teddy said quickly. "Like ginger ale that's been opened too long."

"Exactly," the girl agreed, and a laugh arose to her lips. "No—can't laugh—hurts my head. Where's poor old Hatrack?"

"Over there," Roy said, pointing. "He's down and out."

"Like me," Miss Harper muttered. "Oh, here's Tod. Hello, Tod! Warm weather we're having—" With a sigh the girl fell back.

"Bessie!"

Tod, his face pale, fairly fell from his horse.

"Bessie, for heaven's sake—"

"I'm all right, old thing," the girl whispered. "Only tired. No, not here!"

"Here or any place else!" Tod exclaimed fiercely, and kissed her. Then he turned to Teddy and Roy. "Boys, I can't—" He choked up. "Bessie, here, you see—it isn't known yet, but Bessie and I—we're—"

"He's trying to say we're engaged," Bessie murmured, her eyes still closed. "You always were a poor speechmaker, Tod dear."

Roy stepped forward, his face shining.

"That's great, Tod!" he declared eagerly. "And we're the first to know it! Best wishes! Why, it's like a story—I mean—"

"Don't mind him, he's got the romantics," Teddy said, grinning. "Congratulations, Tod!"

"Thanks, boys," Tod said quietly. "I can't say all I want to now. I suppose you realize what you just did. Later, perhaps—"

"Aw, it was nothing," Teddy faltered, embarrassed in his turn. "We were glad to do it —no, I don't mean just that—but, well—"

"Sign off," Roy chuckled. "Trying to make a bum out of me, hey? How do you feel now, Miss Harper?"

"Like an egg-shake," the girl answered. "Help me up, Tod. I always get a cold from sitting on the grass."

Tod gently helped her to her feet. She stood for a moment, swaying dizzily, and when Tod put out an arm she waved him aside.

"Want to stand in my own shoes. Let's see now—yep, they work." She took a step forward. Then she moved both arms. "Wings all right, too. Well, guess I'm not hurt after all!" She smiled gayly. "My head doesn't count. Movie actresses aren't supposed to have any, you know."

She allowed Tod to wipe the blood from her forehead with his handkerchief, and then, leaning on his arm, she walked a few feet.

"My, what a long distance we rode!" she exclaimed, noticing how far away the camp was. "No one could say I ever shirked a walk, but somehow to-day I don't feel up to it. I wonder—"

"We'll bring the car for you!" Teddy suggested eagerly. "You and Tod wait here. We'll be back right away."

Miss Harper looked at the boy. Then she turned to Roy, who had also dismounted, and who stood watching.

"Teddy—Roy—" her voice faltered. She

took a deep breath, then went on, stronger now. "You may think I haven't been very—well, demonstrative. Perhaps I may have appeared to take your rescue as a matter of course. I hate dramatics. Perhaps it's because I'm an actress that I detest fake gratitude, where the heroine falls down before her deliverer in humility, gushing all over everybody. I do a great deal of kidding. But now I'm serious. I want you to know—" she took a hand of each, and gazed into their faces—"I want you to know that I realize the thing you've done. If that horse had fallen on me—" a shudder passed over her—"I'd have been hash, I guess. It may sound weather-beaten and hackneyed and all that, but—you saved my life. I'm grateful. That's all I'll say. I know you understand the rest. You're the kind of boys who would."

She stood there for a moment, looking at them. They saw that tears were in her eyes. Suddenly she dropped their hands, and laughed.

"Don't get fussed, boys—it's only me! All girls cry at the slightest excuse—didn't you know that? Tod, old fellow, I'm thirsty! I want a big, cool glass of lemonade—with lots of sugar!"

CHAPTER XIX

Off on Location

In the hearts of the movie folk Roy and Teddy Manley were firmly established. The whole camp had seen the rescue, and although they dodged it as much as they could, the boys could not avoid a certain amount of hero-worship.

Tod Jackson said little, but he looked much. As Teddy or Roy would pass him, perhaps on the way to dinner or to see to their ponies, there was a touch on the arm, a hand flung about the shoulders, that told them, more strongly than any words, how the actor felt. They had saved the girl he loved. They had made a friend for life.

Bessie Harper refused to be babied just because she had "kissed a horse," and insisted on going on with the picture. Her injury was not serious, the only ill effect being a bad headache.

"That, and a certain sense of injustice," she explained. "To think that old plug would up and run away with me! I'll never trust another horse as long as I live. They're too uncertain."

159

"If that break didn't look real I'll go back to the farm," Sam vowed. "Miss Harper, you done it wonderful. Monkeys, it was great! And those boys ought to get a Carnegie medal. By golly, I'll recommend them for one! I have an uncle who used to work for a man who's wife was very intimate with Carnegie's sister-in-law. I'll write to him and tell him about it. Yes sir, boys, we'll have a medal for you!"

"No thanks," Teddy laughed. "If I got a medal I'd have to wear it on a coat, and I don't like to wear a coat. So no medal. We'll ride for you instead."

Work was called off for the remainder of the day, but on the following morning the shots were resumed. Teddy, on Flash, was taken in a "pony express" start, and then several long views of him burning up the Trail were filmed. That afternoon three more horses arrived from Eagles, followed by a flivver which carried back the men who drove them. There was a road that lead from Big Bison Trail to the town, but it was very roundabout, and it was a good three days' journey.

"Now we take the scenes we really came after," Tod explained to Teddy and Roy. "Reckon these ponies will carry us all right, won't they? Don't look much like poor Spindle-shanks." The horse that had run away with Miss Harper had been put on the "ineligible list."

The boys looked at the newly arrived bron-cos admiringly. They were wonderful steeds.

"They'll take you any place," Roy declared. "But what are you going to use them for?"

"We'll hit the real Trail now," Tod said. "You boys ever been past those mountains?"

They said they had not.

"Well, the man who planned this trip told me we'd get some real country back there. To-morrow we'll start. Sam, Lem, Break, you two, and myself. Teddy, I'm depending on you to give us some snappy action."

"Do my best," Teddy responded. "Anything short of jumping over cliffs."

"Well, we'll hardly ask you to do that. Roy, you rate a close-up. Think you can stand it?"

"If the camera can," Roy laughed. "I'll be a little bit of local color. You mean we're all go-ing to ride up past the mountains and then the pictures will be taken there?"

"That's it. Or wait! I have a better idea! Instead of all of us going together, suppose you two boys go on ahead and select a good location? You know more about the West than we do. Just follow the Trail—it narrows off about six miles away, our man said. Then when you get to a spot that presents picture possibilities, you wait for us there. That'll save time. Break O'Day can go with you—he's seen enough of this game to know when he hits location.

Hey, Break,'' Tod raised his voice to a shout. ''Come here a second, will you?''

The flaps of one of the tents parted, and Break stuck his head out. He was evidently in the process of eating, for the Adam's apple was bobbing frantically. Then it took one deep dive, as though it had been swallowed, and resumed normalcy.

''Want me?'' Break asked casually, when this gastronomic feat had been accomplished.

''Yes. You and Teddy and Roy are going to take a trip to-morrow. Up the Trail.''

''Are we?'' The youth's eyes lighted and he stepped out, his head just missing the top of the tent door. ''That'll be great! I like to be up an' doing. That's just what I need—action. Been too slow all my life. What's the dope?''

''You three are to go out on location. We'll follow along later. Bessie and Miss de Lisle will stay here, and so will the others—I mean the three new men and the cooks. We'll be gone only two days—at the most three. After that we'll hit for home.''

''New York?'' Break asked, a smile coming over his face.

''That very same village. Anxious to get back?''

''Um! It's nice out here—the trees, the air, the mountains, the rest of it. But I don't know —there's something about Broadway. It gets you here.'' He placed his hand over his heart.

The boy was perfectly serious, but Teddy had to turn aside to conceal a grin. Break could not help being funny. "You remember what you promised me, Tod?" he asked.

"I couldn't forget it," Tod answered, chuckling. "Break, you'll be a full-fledged comedian before a year is up."

"Will I?" his face fairly shone. "Me, an actor! Look! Here's my cards, with Pithican-thropy written on them." With a quick motion he tossed them high in the air. "Good-bye, Pithy! You have proven a false master! I'll serve you no longer! That ape I lost was a blessing in disguise. I shall never forget him. But now he has departed to the port of missing ships. Hey! what you laughin' at?"

"Nothing," Tod answered, struggling to get his breath. "Get—get ready, Break. We leave early in the morning. I—excuse me—my throat—"

He made a beeline for the tent.

"Now I wonder what's eatin' him?" Break asked in a puzzled tone. "I didn't know he had a sore throat."

"Probably swallowed the wrong way," Teddy replied, biting his lips. With an effort he recovered his gravity. He was afraid to look at Roy, for fear he, too, would lose control of himself and be forced to flee after Tod. "Yes, you're a full-fledged actor, Break. Good luck to you! Come on, Roy, we've got to get our stuff together.''

Break looked after them wondering. They, too, seemed to have throat trouble. He shook his head, and walked away.

The start for the upper part of Big Bison Trail was made early the next day under a cloudless sky. The whole company was awake to watch the three riders off, and Miss Harper insisted on seeing that they had enough things to keep them warm.

"It gets cold at night,'' she said anxiously. "Don't you want several blankets apiece?''

"Not us,'' Roy said, smiling. "It won't be the first time we've camped out, you know.''

"You needn't fear for them, Bessie,'' Tod declared. "They were born in the West. We Easterners are just beginners out here.''

"But for all of that, we appreciate your solicitude,'' Break said sincerely. "I, myself, am but a tenderfoot—or feet. Oh, well, let it lay as it was first. Anyway—''

"Stick to that horse, Break!'' Tod called out, a grin on his face. "Don't let him throw you!''

Roy led the way out of camp, forestalling Break's reply.

The three had soon left the tents behind and were headed for the mountains. For a long while they rode silently, even Break O'Day keeping strangely quiet. Then, suddenly, he jumped as though a bee had stung him.

"Golly, we forgot!" he exclaimed. "What are we ever going to do? And it's all my fault! Well, I'm sorry, fellows!"

"What the mischief?" Teddy said in wonderment, staring at their companion. "Why the worry, Break?"

"We forgot to say where we'd meet them!" the youth groaned. "Oh, junks, isn't that hard luck! What'll we do now?"

"Don't let that bother you," Roy laughed. "We fixed that up. All we do is pick a good spot and wait. Don't you know this is a trail we're on?"

"Like a street, hey?" Break returned, his face brightening. "You walk up Fifth Avenue and tell a friend you'll wait for him somewhere around the Library. That the idea?"

"That's it," Teddy replied. "Though if what I hear about New York is true, the friend would have a hard job finding you. But there're not *quite* so many people out here. We'll find Tod all right."

"Well, I'm glad of that," Break sighed. "This is a pretty big country—a pretty big country. There's so much of everything. But I like it fine. It got me a job at last!"

CHAPTER XX

THE three riders followed the narrow Trail through the mountains, now dipping deep between the crags where a cool mist lay, now rising high above the plain that spread out behind them. At last, toward evening, they came upon a scene which left the mind stunned and gasping for adjectives. Big Bison Trail widened like a generous palm at the end of a dainty wrist. On the right a sloping cliff cut the sky in half. On the left a gentle incline led down to a sparkling river, like a silver thread on brown moss. Directly to the front were huge rocks, the color of old iron.

"This," said Roy, as he stood in contemplation, "is it!"

His two companions nodded. There was no need to ask him for an explanation. The thought was in the minds of all three riders that they had come to the spot they had been looking for—a perfect setting for a picture.

"Tod will like this," Teddy said musingly. "The cameras will be set over there, to get those rocks for a background. The action can take

166

place on this plateau. It's like a stage."

"You boys been in this business long?"
Break inquired, a look of surprise on his face.

"Not long," Teddy answered with a laugh.
"Should say about three days."

"Three days!" Break whistled long and low.
"How come you pick locations like this? Me,
I'm not so good at location hunting, but I been
around movies long enough to know a good one
when I see it. And, believe me, this here is a
piperino! Look at that cliff with the sky behind it! And the river down there! Baby!
Couldn't be better if it had been painted. Wait
till Sam and Tod see it. They'll go batty over
it."

The horses were soon unsaddled, given water,
and picketed a short distance down the Trail,
and preparations were made for spending the
night. Tod was not expected until the next day,
and there was nothing to do but rest. After
supper was over, the three threw themselves
down by the fire. It was still daylight, though
the sun was out of sight, and streaks of blue and
gold striped the sky. Break puffed thoughtfully
on a cigarette, knees drawn up under his chin,
his long legs making a perfect inverted V.

"Yes," he said, "I'm sure glad I lost that
baboon. If I hadn't things would've been different—a lot different. I wouldn't ever have
had a chance to be an actor. I'd have collected
the money for the rent of the monk, taken him

back, and gone my own silly way. Instead, I'm set now for life—or I hope so. Yea, bo, I'm certainly glad I lost my monk!"

Roy nodded. He was not thinking so much about the ape as he was of the occurrences since Teddy had seen the creature in that cabin. But the air was soft and pleasant, and thoughts were hazy to-night. Roy tilted back his head and looked up the cliff at the edge of the Trail. The top was enveloped in a sort of red mist, as though the sun were shining through a ruby fog.

"Wonder how high that is?" he mused, but he did not bother to express his thought. Suddenly a stone became dislodged from somewhere up on the heights and came tumbling down, beating an eccentric tattoo on the hard ground. Roy started and opened his eyes wide.

"Mountain goat," Teddy grinned. "Been dreaming again? I was watching you. You sat there with your eyes half-closed and a look on your face as if the wonders of the world were made for your benefit."

"Maybe they were," Break interrupted. "As well as for anyone else."

"I was thinking," Roy answered evenly, "of—"

Crash!

Another rock leaped down the mountain, bounding like a live thing.

"What the mischief!" Teddy exclaimed, and

started to his feet. "Some one's heaving stones at us!"

"Don't they sometimes fall without having been thrown?" Break asked, his only reaction to the episode being the removal of the cigarette from his mouth.

"Sure," Roy said easily. "They rattle down all by themselves. Be seated, brother mine. There is no cause for alarm."

"Think I don't know that?" Teddy answered testily. "Guess I can stretch when I want to, can't I? Let the whole mountain fall. Won't worry me."

As if in obedience to his suggestion, a third crash sounded, this one much louder than the others. Now all three boys were on their feet, watching a cloud of dust far up the mountainside.

"Something's coming!" Roy shouted "Looks like a boulder rolling along!"

"No—can't be—it's stopped! Here it comes again!" Teddy was peering fixedly up toward the top of the cliff. "Isn't that silly! Jimminy! Whatever it is, it's sure making enough noise! Listen! Is that yelling?"

The three boys strained their ears. Then, faintly above the noise of the crashes, sounded a voice.

"It's a man falling down!" Roy exclaimed. "He's calling for help. See that? He caught a tree, then lost his grip and shoots down again

Golly, what a fall! He'll be mincemeat by the time he gets here!''

"Sure it's a man?" Break wanted to know. "It might be an animal."

"Animals don't speak English," Roy said grimly. "It's a man, all right. If he keeps that course he'll hit just about where we are. Unless he stops himself. Lucky there's lots of bushes on that mountain. There he is! He's caught hold! Now he's all right! Let's get him, Teddy. We can climb that. Hurry! He might —oh, golly, here he comes again! He's lost now! All we can do is to pick up the pieces!"

The tumbling figure was approaching the bottom, where the boys stood. In another moment he would be on them.

"Get back!" Roy shouted. "There's a young landslide ahead of him! We'll be beaned if we stay here! Won't do any good to catch him— we couldn't, anyhow! He'll slow up before he hits bottom."

That was what happened. Ten feet above the level ground the tumbler came to a stop. The mountain sloped gradually, and as the figure came to rest the three boys sprang forward.

"He's killed sure," Teddy said in a low voice. "What a fall!"

They reached the form that lay silent just below a clump of bushes. Teddy bent and turned the figure over. Then he gave a cry of astonishment.

It was a man, an old man, and his garments were nearly ripped off him. Blood was streaming from many cuts about his face and body. His white beard was matted with dirt. His eyes were closed and his bushy eyebrows were contracted, as though with pain.

"For the love of Pete!" Teddy breathed. "I know him!"

"He won't be much to know unless we get him out of here quick," Break said decidedly. Strangely enough, in an emergency, he seemed to lose his ungainliness and become a reliable man. "We've got to give him some water. Teddy, run down and grab your canteen. Roy and I will cart him out of this."

Carefully Break and Roy carried the unconscious man down to the camp. Teddy, who had removed the top from his canteen, poured a few drops of water between the thin lips.

"Heart's beating," Roy declared. "He's alive, anyway, and it's a wonder he is. A man of his age falling down that mountain! He must be at least seventy. Don't let him choke on that water, Teddy."

Now the figure shuddered convulsively, and the two skinny hands weakly seized the canteen. With his eyes still closed, the man drank deeply.

"Must have been lost," Break muttered. "Poor old geezer!"

Teddy, heedful of the consequences of allowing a very thirsty man to drink too fast, pulled the canteen away gently. Then the eyes opened, and the lips moved.

"You'll be all right," Teddy said soothingly. "Just lie still. Here—take it easy now, and we'll let you have some more water in a minute."

The man nodded, and pointed to his throat, then to the ground. Roy, rightly interpreting, raised his head so he could drink more easily. After a moment the old man ceased swallowing and sighed deeply. Then, for the first time, he noticed Teddy.

"You—you—" he faltered, and coughed.

"Yes, I know you," Teddy replied soothingly. "You live in Los Dipono, don't you?"

The man nodded silently. Teddy turned his head toward Roy and Break.

"He's the man I bought Belle's stuffed bear from—the man Nick told me about. What on earth can he be doing away out here?"

"Time enough to find that out later," Roy remarked. "The thing to do now is to see how badly he's hurt. Mister," he said loudly, "where are you injured? Head? Legs? Arms?"

The old man looked up at him.

"Generally," he said, and grinned weakly.

"The game old bird!" Break exclaimed in admiration. "Pop, we'll have you fixed up in a jiffy! Let's get his clothes off, boys, and lay him on a blanket. Not much clothes left to take off. Easy, Pop, we sha'n't hurt you any more than we have to. We want to bathe those cuts of yours. Great Cæsar, he looks like he'd been through a meat-chopper!''

Except for an occasional groan, the man kept silence while the boys ministered to his hurts. They found that no bones were broken, for a wonder, although some of the cuts were deep and ugly. But at last they were bound up with torn handkerchiefs and parts of Break's white shirt, and the bleeding stopped. The blanket was wrapped about the man's shoulders, and food was given him. From the way he ate, it was easy to see that he had been on a starvation diet for some days.

Not until he was resting easily did his rescuers press him for his story. By that time full night had set in, and the campfire was their only source of light.

CHAPTER XXI

The Birthmark

For some moments the old man sat staring with unseeing eyes into the flames. Perhaps he was thinking of the miracle that had happened to him, the extraordinary good fortune that allowed him to sit here swathed in a blanket, near the comforting warmth, instead of lying bruised, broken, and silent against some tree trunk. He hunched his broad, bony shoulders and raised his head to the stars.

"It's good," he said slowly, "to be livin'."

Roy glanced at him quickly. Then the old man lowered his eyes and Roy saw they were sparkling, bright, the blue merry eyes of contented old age. The boy smiled.

"Guess we all agree there," he said heartily. "You had a narrow escape. Did I understand you to say you knew my brother?"

"This your brother?" the man asked, turning to Teddy. Without waiting for an answer he went on: "Never mind. I see him. You're as alike as two peas in a pod."

Break O'Day started and wrinkled his brows.

174

Teddy was a distinct blond. Roy was taller, much darker.

"Oh, I don't mean just looks," the man added quickly. "They don't count for much. I mean somethin' else. They have the same feelin'." He hesitated a moment. Then: "Don't suppose anyone's got a pipe?"

"Got some cigarettes," Break offered, holding out a package. The old man took one and lit it gingerly. "Never did take to these things much, but in a pinch I reckon they'll have to do. Thanks. Sure I know the youngster."

Teddy nodded. "I remember you, sir. I bought a stuffed bear from you in Los Dipono. You're a taxidermist, aren't you?"

"Who, me?" The blue eyes stared widely. "Nope. Methodist. I stuff animals fer a livin'. Name's Hank Wall. Say, I ain't thanked you, boys, fer what you done fer me. I'm plumb grateful." He gazed at each in turn and bent his head slightly. "Plumb grateful! I'm an old man, an' maybe most people would figger I wasn't worth botherin' about. But I am."

"Certainly you are," Teddy interrupted. "How do you feel now? Anything we can do for you?"

"You done enough," Hank Wall answered graciously. "All I want now is rest. I came out here to get in the pitchers."

"Pictures?" Break said excitedly. "You mean the moving pictures?"

"Sure do! I'm a type! Feller came into my shop a week ago and told me. So I come out to get my pitcher took. Where are the actors?"

"Here are a few of 'em," Break declared proudly. "The others are coming along to-morrow. I'm a comedian."

"Uh-huh," Hank said laconically. "You look it. Say, let's see you swally again, will yuh?"

"What? Swallow? What for?" Break looked at the man curiously. "You're all right —I mean your head don't feel queer, does it?"

"No. I ain't crazy, neither. You have the biggest Adam's apple I ever see." Teddy and Roy turned quickly and stared hard at the river below. Their shoulders were shaking strangely. "But never mind that now," the old man continued. "You're actors, hey? Well, ain't that the beatenest! I fall plumb into a nest of 'em. Say—" he turned to Teddy "how come you're an actor? Thought you was on a ranch near Eagles."

"I am. We're just helping the picture company out," Teddy explained. "We're really not actors—at least, Roy and I aren't."

"That's good. Say, you want to buy any more stuffed animals? I got a humdinger now. Feller what shot it sold it to me an' I stuffed it. Want to buy it?"

"Well, I don't believe so," Teddy replied. "What kind of an animal?"

Hank drew deep on the cigarette before he answered.

"Don't rightly know," he said. "Looks kinda like a man, only it's all hairy. Gorilla, I reckon."

"A gorilla!" Break O'Day jumped as though he had been stung. "Where is it? Where'd you get it. Gee whillikins, fellows, I'll bet—" He stopped suddenly. Hank was staring eagerly at his throat. Break flushed and went on more quietly. "I can't help it if my Adam's apple is large, Mr. Wall. I wish you wouldn't stare like that."

"Scuse me, son," Hank said apologetically. "I didn't mean to hurt your feelin's. Reckon I couldn't help it. But what's that you said?"

"I asked you where you got the baboon."

"Baboon? Well, maybe. Feller sold it to me last week. He shot it. My, it was large! Gonna make a fine piece, boys, when it's finished! Think you want to buy it?"

"It's mine," Break declared. "It's my ape. I bought him all the way out here to rent him to the moving picture people—to Tod Jackson. And now he's dead!"

"Was he a pet, son?" Hank inquired sadly.

"Not him," Break said, with a little laugh. "For a while he was my meal ticket. But I guess he got punched once too often. You're welcome to him. Well, well! So that's where old Pithy ended! Anyway, I'm glad to know he's in safe hands. He won't scare anybody else, I guess.''

"He'll be a work of art," Hank Wall exclaimed warmly. "I'll take special care with him, son. He'll be my—my masterpiece. You don't need to grieve for him. He'll look better when I finish than he did when he was alive. So he was goin' in the pitchers too! Ain't this a funny world? I leave my business to ride forty miles out here, fall off my bronc, an' meet the actors an' the owner of my gorilla! Who ṣays nothin' don't happen in the West?''

"Not me," Break said firmly. "Things have been happening to me ever since I arrived here. You say you fell off a horse, Mr. Wall?''

"That's what! Son," this ,to Teddy, "that fire's burnin' low. When you get my age the spring ain't as warm as it used to be—specially after tumblin' down a mountain. Thanks!'' Teddy had thrown some logs on the blaze, and it flamed up. "Yea, my bronc stumbled up there on the mountain an' sent me over his head. Pete knows where he is by this time. Home, maybe. He's a fast pony.''

Hank flicked his cigarette into the air. "So the pitcher people are comin' out to-morrow! Be all right to stay with you folks to-night? I feel kinda sore and—''

"Certainly you'll stay!" Teddy declared firmly. "You're a friend of Nick Looker's

aren't you? He told me about you. That's
how I found your shop.''

"Friend? I knowed Nick Looker ever since
he was born!'' Hank exclaimed. "So you an'
him are pals, hey? Then I guess you're all
right. Nick always was my favorite kid. I remember when he was four years old he used
to come toddlin' around my place askin' for
candy. I kept a general store then.''

"You remember when he was four years
old?'' Roy repeated eagerly. He glanced
quickly toward his brother. "Don't suppose
you could remember the day he was born, could
you?''

Teddy and Roy leaned forward, waiting for
the old man to speak. His eyes brightened,
and he snapped his fingers loudly.

"Remember it? Son, I'll never forget it as
long as I live! It was on Christmas day, just
—let's see now—twenty-six—no twenty-seven
years ago! The year of the big blizzard. Snow!
I never see anything like it before nor since!
Remember it? Son, I remember it like it was
yesterday!''

"But how could you tell that Nick Looker
was the particular baby born then?'' Teddy
asked tensely. "It's so long ago that maybe
this Nick Looker is some one else!''

"Some one else? I don't rightly understand
you. The Lookers lived four doors away from
me. On Christmas day Mr. Looker—Nick's

father—come rushin' over an' told me he'd just got a Christmas present. So I followed him to the house, ploughin' through snow six feet deep. An' there was Nick—as purty a baby as you'd ever want to see, a-squawlin' and a-squawkin'. Some Christmas present, hey? I can just see him now, the little snoozer—lookin' up at me, an' then tryin' to turn over on his face. Me, I turned him over! He had a birthmark right between the shoulder-blades, too.''

''A birthmark?'' Roy asked excitedly. ''A birthmark, Mr. Wall? What kind? Are you sure?''

''Course I'm sure! Didn't I see it? Don't Nick bear it to this day—though I doubt if he knows it. A little black mark like a star. Mrs. Looker wanted to call him Star, but the old man sat on that idea quick. Huh! Callin' old man Looker's kid Star 'cause he was born on Christmas an' had one on him!''

''Listen!'' Roy exclaimed, and got to his feet. ''what you're saying is important—mighty important, Mr. Wall. It happens that Nick has to prove his identity in order to get some money that his uncle left him. Understand me? You say he has a birthmark on him, a black star. Have you ever seen that mark since the day he was born?''

''No!'' Hank Wall shook his head decidely. ''I ain't. Never even seen Nick in swimmin'.

But I know the mark's there, all right. Birthmarks don't come off. I had an aunt once that had one on the end of her nose. Yes sir, right plumb on the end of her nose! An' she wore it till the day she died. That was Aunt Petronilla. Right on the end of her nose! Now—"

"Listen," Roy said again. "You've got to come home with us when the pictures are finished. You've got to swear to what you've told us. Will you do that?"

"Certainly will! Swear my dyin' oath! It's true, every word!"

"Teddy," Roy turned to his brother, eyes shining, "we've gotten Nick's money for him! Now the court will have to admit he's Nick Looker! And the proof fell down the mountain right into our hands!"

CHAPTER XXII

PLANNING A SURPRISE

WHEN it was finally brought home to Hank Wall that he could assist his old friend Nick Looker in getting his legacy, the old man was anxious to start immediately for home.

"Seems like we're wastin' time settin' round here," he demurred. "I come out here to go in the pitchers, but since this turned up I've kinda lost interest in the other. Jinks! I'd like to go right now to the court house an' tell that judge what's what! Sayin' Nick Looker is some one else!"

"Plenty of time for that," Roy said, smiling. "There are a few thing to be attended to first. And since you traveled so far to see the moving picture people, you might as well do it, Mr. Wall."

"Long, far, an' hard, I traveled," Hank Wall mused. "Didn't have much food either. Then to-day my water ran out just as I reached the start of the Trail. Knew I could get some when I reached the river down there, so I kept on. Then my pony stumbled, an' I guess you know the rest."

182

"How did you know we were out on Big
Bison Trail?" Break asked.

"Why, this here feller told me. I heard that
a pitcher company was over to Eagles, an' when
I found out they was lookin' for actors I rid
there. Told you I was a type, didn't I? Well,
when I got to Eagles I asked questions, an' the
feller said the company was headed fer the
Trail. So out I come."

"Who do you mean by 'the feller'?" Teddy
inquired. "Who told you we were here, Mr.
Wall?"

"A tall, light-haired geezer. Looked like an
Easterner to me. Him an' some short feller
were hangin' round the station. Funny, when
I asked them about the pitcher company the
short feller kind of got flustered an' his friend
laughed. Say, is your name Manley?" he had
turned suddenly to Teddy.

"Yes, it is. I thought you knew. Why?"

"Well, this here light-haired feller was talkin'
to his pal when I come up. They was standin'
near the station, by that hitchin' rail, an' when
I walked over to ask 'em about the pitchers the
tall feller said somethin' about the Manley
boys, an' that they were glad you were out of
the way fer a while. Then they both laughed."

Roy looked at his brother, a question in his
eyes. The fire burned low, but neither paid
much attention to it. Break O'Day was an
absorbed listener, sitting silently, now and then

swallowing convulsively. It seemed to him that a story was being enacted before his eyes. The flames threw weired shadows on the ground, and the lanky youth shivered delightedly. The charms of New York were fast fading under the spell of the Western night.

Teddy was the first to express the thought that was in the mind of each.

"Pettit and that actor," he said slowly. "What do you make of it, Roy?"

"You say they spoke of our being out of the way?" Roy asked Hank Wall. "Then they laughed?"

"Yes, that's what. When I told 'em I was coming out to the Trail too, they kinda snickered. Somehow, I didn't take to them two!"

"And neither do we!" Teddy said forcibly. "Roy, there something up. Pettit has been to see Nick again, I'll lay money on it." The boy arose and walked up and down in front of the fire. "He's a crook, and nothing less. Glad we're out of the way, is he? Well, by golly, we'll see about that! The will of Nick's uncle won't be offered for probate until next week. When it is, we'll be there! Hey, Roy?"

"With bells on," Roy added grimly. "We'll see what that fake Nick Looker has to say when we trot out Mr. Wall's story! He'll eat pretty small apples then, I'll bet!"

"Me—I'll be in court?" the old man demanded, his eyes shining. "Cricky, that's good!

That's plumb good! I like court. I know all
about it, too. Back in eighty-six I testified in
a murder case. Me, I was the state's witness.''
He raised his head proudly and made as if to
stand up. Then he winced as he pulled on a
sore muscle and gave up the attempt. But
the gleam in his eyes was still unquenched.
''They all leaned forward in their chairs when
I testified, they did,'' he went on eagerly.
''Then a smart lawyer kept askin' me questions,
but he couldn't catch me. No sir! I was too
quick for him.''

''You'll have another day in court,'' Teddy
declared excitedly. ''Hope these movie shots
won't take too long. I'm anxious to get back
to help Nick. The money means a lot to him.
So they're glad we're out of the way, are they?
Well, we'll see!''

''Are you going to get his money for him?''
Break inquired. He hugged his knees with his
long arms and grinned. ''Wasn't it fortunate
we stopped here for the night? A trick of fate.
Some day I'm going to write a play about this,
for the movies. Maybe I'll act in it, too. Why,
Mr. Wall fell right in your arms, didn't he?
Golly, I wish it had happened to me! But I
can't complain. I've had enough adventures
since I came out here with the ape. Say, Mr.
Wall, maybe I'll buy Pithy from you, as a souvenir. That is, if Tod'll advance the money
out of my salary. Say, I want to go to court

with you and see the finish of this thing! Can I? Will you let me?"

"Glad to have you, Break," Roy said warmly. "Besides, you're a witness to Mr. Wall's story, you know. You may have to be there."

Teddy, glancing over at the old man, noticed that the white head was beginning to fall forward. He made a sign to Roy, and together the two boys laid the old man on a blanket and wrapped him well with two others. He slept heavily, the sleep of exhaustion, his huge, bony frame completely relaxed.

"He'll be a different person in the morning," Roy declared, looking down at the silent figure. "Nice old fellow, isn't he? Game as they make 'em. Think of riding forty miles at his age! Well, it's lucky for us he did. Now we've got Pettit where the hair is short. Boy, I'm tired! Do you realize it must be nearly eleven o'clock? We've been gassing away here for a good two hours. Gooda-night, gentlemans!" and he shrugged his shoulders and threw out his hands in Italian fashion.

Roy had given his blanket to their visitor, so he and Teddy shared the latter's coverings. Soon there were those soft, homely sounds that tell of men asleep—an occasional deep breath, a sigh as some one shifts from one side to the other, perhaps the muttering of a few disconnected words. But for the most part there was deep silence.

The fire flickered, went out. The river, below, murmured sleepily. The night stars winked solemnly onward. A hushed waiting. The heavy hours just before dawn. The single note of a catbird. Streaks of dull gray. Morning.

Tod and the others arrived at mid-day. They had started the evening before and had covered a good deal of ground before halting. At Tod's suggestion they had broken camp at daylight, and hence their arrival had been a few hours earlier than the boys had expected.

Hank Wall was as excited as a child when he saw them ride up. Although he had awakened very stiff in limb and muscle, yet there were no really ill effects of his terrible fall. Indeed, he seemed to have forgotten it entirely, and when Teddy attempted to explain to Tod how they had come upon him he interrupted so frequently that Teddy gave up.

"So I'm seein' the real thing in the flesh and not just the pitchers in the Grand The-a-ter Palace at home!" he said over and over.

Later, when the old man had quieted down somewhat, the story of his connection with Nick Looker's inheritance was told.

Tod was as happy as were the boys over the turn affairs had taken. He agreed with Teddy and Roy that this proof would be enough to establish Nick's identity to the satisfaction of any court.

"And I want to be there when it's done," he

added. "If for nothing else than to see our "actor" friend get what he deserves. Now we'll take these shots as quickly as possible. We may be able to finish them all in two or three days and start back. Yes, yes, Mr. Wall, we can use you. You come along home with us and we'll fit you in some place. In fact, we'll use you right here. Lem, get your camera set up. Boys, you picked a wonderful location—wonderful! This is what we came West for, to Big Bison Trail. Isn't this great, Sam? Wait till the boss sees the prints of this! Why, it's perfect. You'd better get some long shots first. Hadn't he, Sam? Then we can shoot Teddy on his horse rounding that turn down there. All right, Sam, I guess you know what to do better than I."

The director nodded and gave his instructions. The rest of that day and the two to follow were devoted to work—hard work. Roy and Teddy were filmed time and time again until Sam was finally satisfied that the pictures were right. Then they took a close up of Mr. Wall. The old gentleman sat fascinated, scarcely daring to breathe, as the camera turned. Then Tod's action was shot, and finally, just as the last bit of sunlight disappeared, Sam called out: "Cut!"

The pictures were finished. "Big Bison Trail" was packed in round tin boxes, to be taken to New York for the edification of Easterners. Teddy and Roy Manley had done their parts. Those whom they would never see would see them on the screen. The "movies" were over. Early the next morning the company started back, Hank Wall riding double with Break O'Day.

CHAPTER XXIII

A Blot of Ink

The riders traveled more slowly toward the moving picture camp than they had away from it, partly because the party was larger, which always delays matters, and partly because of Hank Wall. Frequent shifts had to be made, so that one horse would not bear the burden of carrying two men for the whole journey.

They arrived in the "tent city," as Teddy called it, long after dusk had fallen. Bessie Harper was delighted to learn that the trip was a success, as far as pictures went, and when she heard about the finding of Hank Wall she insisted that he tell her the whole story.

"Just make believe you're on the witness stand now," she coaxed, and the old man told her the tale almost in the very same words he had related it before. Bessie watched the faces of Teddy and Roy while Hank talked, and later she asked them if his story checked with the one they had heard.

"Exactly," Roy answered. "So that's why you were so anxious to have him tell it! Miss Harper, that was clever!"

"Oh, well, I wouldn't go so far as to say that," the actress laughed. "But you see Mr. Wall is rather old, and sometimes aged people get queer ideas. But I think he's got his part down pat. He may be old, but he's got a young brain."

Teddy and Roy stayed over night at the movie camp, but the next morning decided to start for the X Bar X. Tod said the company was going to break camp that day, anyway, since the pictures were finished, and get to Eagles as soon as possible.

"These scenes have got to reach New York," he explained. "The boss is waiting for them. So you two boys ride on as soon as you want to, and we'll follow as quickly as we can get the stuff packed up. You know we travel in autos, and we may reach Eagles almost as soon as you do."

Teddy, looking at Star and Flash, shook his head at this. Autos were all right, but in this country a good bronco had it on them coming and going. Still, they were a real necessity for ladies—and old men. Thus it was that Hank Wall was easily prevailed upon to ride back with the company instead of "forking a bronco." So amid shouted farewells the two boys left alone.

Halfway home the fair weather deserted them, and a long, steady drizzle set in, making the ride very uncomfortable. But both Teddy and Roy felt that it would be unwise to halt because of this, and, pulling their sombreros low over their eyes, they rode on.

"Lucky this held off as long as it did," Teddy remarked, as he shifted in his saddle. "We'd have been in a fine fix if it had rained while the pictures were being taken. Perhaps we would never have gone up the Trail, and then we'd never have found Hank Wall."

"Right," Roy answered laconically. He spoke no more for some minutes. Then: "Teddy, I've been thinking. Why do you suppose Pettit said he was glad to have us out of the way?"

Teddy shrugged his shoulders. "Can't say. I suppose it had something to do with Nick and his money. I only hope he hasn't gotten Nick to assign his claim by pretending that his case is hopeless. Nick would be likely to do that, too. He was pretty badly worried when we left. He'd be glad to get it off his hands."

"You mean that Pettit might offer him, say, a thousand to assign his rights to that actor?" Roy demanded, a note of excitement creeping into his voice. "Snakes, Teddy, I never thought of that! Suppose he's already done, it? All our work done for nothing. Hank Wall's testimony won't do a bit of good! Jimminy, I—"

"Cool off, Roy, my lad," Teddy chuckled. "Up to your old tricks again, aren't you? I merely suggested that as a possibility. Chances

are that nothing like that will happen at all.
Nick has got some sense. Ugh, this rain!''
They plodded on. ''I'll bet Nick won't let Pettit
come near the place, Roy. And dad knows about
that money-grabbing lawyer, too. Surely Nick
would ask dad's opinion before doing anything
rash.''

Roy shook his head.

''I'm not so certain of that, Teddy. Nick is
an independent sort of cuss. He hates to wait
for anything. Wish you hadn't mentioned that.
You've got me worried.''

''Oh, fish-cakes! Snap out of it! Nick isn't
as dumb as you think he is.''

''Not dumb, Teddy, but—well, emotional.
Now if it were Gus Tripp, I wouldn't give that
lawyer an outside chance against him. Gus
would hang on till the last ball was pitched. But
Nick's different. Well, here's hoping we get
there in time. Let's see if we can make some
speed.''

Teddy glanced at his brother, but said nothing. He knew the futility of trying to convince
him of anything when he was in this mood.

Teddy, himself, was rather anxious about the
whole affair, but wisely he did not confess his
fears to Roy. It seemed perfectly probable to
him that Pettit had succeeded in tricking Nick
into releasing his claim. At first he had not
thought much about it, the words coming to his
lips almost before he realized that he had said

them. But now he mulled the situation over as he rode along, and he felt a growing certainty that Nick had given up, that they would arrive at the X Bar X too late. Unconsciously he touched his heels to Flash's sides, and the two boys galloped through the rain.

Actually, things seemed to be breaking too well. It was a streak of pure luck that they had come upon Hank Wall when they did, and it was more than luck that had enabled the old man to live after such a fall and be able to come to Los Dipono to testify. Of course he was not there yet, but he would soon be, in the natural course of events, and Teddy felt positive that his testimony would clinch the legacy for Nick—if it were not too late. If their luck would only hold!

They came to the river where Teddy's horse had come so near to being buried in the quicksand. This time, by common consent, they crossed at the ford. The rain had swelled the stream slightly, so that their crossing was not so easy as it might have been, but they got over safely and started on the home stretch. As they neared the familiar landmarks excitement rose in the breasts of the two riders. Their mid-day meal was a sketchy affair, taking not more than fifteen minutes. Then into the saddle again, and onward.

The rain had changed from a drizzle to a blinding downpour. The boys could hardly see ten feet ahead of them, but the trail was well known to both, and they had no fear of getting lost. They urged the ponies on recklessly. Perhaps it was illogical to imagine haste could avail them anything at this late date, but at least it relieved their feelings to know they were approaching the scene of action as fast as they could.

"Hope Nick's at the ranch when we come in," Roy said, breathing hard. The ride had been long and tiresome, and the riders, as well as the broncos, were feeling the effects of it. "If he is, don't say anything to him about that suggestion of yours. We'll have to sound him out."

"What for? If he's done it, it's too late, and the sooner we find out the better. Hang that Pettit, anyhow! The shyster! I hope he gets socked good and plenty—trying to do a man he never saw before out of his money. And that fake actor is just as bad. If Nick hasn't signed anything, there'll be hot doings in court when Pettit and his friend try to prove their claim!"

"Well, it won't be long now!" Roy said excitedly. "Here we are!"

For a moment the rain ceased. Ahead of them the boys saw the outlines of the X Bar X buildings.

"Home!" Teddy shouted. "Step on it, Roy!"

Impelled by a vague impulse that speed was now the essential thing, the riders raced over the prairie. Breathless, panting, covered with foam, the horses dashed into the yard of the Manley ranch.

The first person the boys saw was Gus Tripp.

"Gus!" Teddy yelled, springing from his horse, "where's Nick?"

"Hello, boys! You sure must be soaked! How'd the pictures turn out?"

"Never mind that now! Where's Nick Looker?" Both boys were on foot now, running toward the cowboy, who stood near the corral.

"Nick? Why, he's in the bunkhouse. He's busy, I think. Got some stranger with him. Tall, light-haired bird. Why?"

"Tell you later!"

Splashing through the mud, the brothers ran toward the door of the bunkhouse. Reaching it, they threw it open and burst in.

In the semi-darkness of the shack they made out two forms bending over a table. One of them was Nick. The other was Pettit. Then Roy saw that Nick had a pen in his hand and that his forearm rested on the table. As the boys sprang forward the pen scratched over the paper.

"Nick! Hey, Nick, stop that!" yelled Teddy.

"Nick!" Roy shouted. "Nick! Don't sign that!" His momentum carried him forward, and he fell against the cowboy, sending the pen to the floor amid a shower of black drops. Roy reached out his hand eagerly and seized the paper.

The boys saw that it was a legal document, closely written. At the foot of it, in a long, scrawling hand, was written in ink: "Nicholas A. L—" That was all. The remainder was a blot of ink. They had come just in time!

CHAPTER XXIV

In Court

Pettit, his face twisted with rage, seized Roy by the arm.

"You country hick!" he snarled, "I'll—"

"You'll let go of my arm, first. Quick!" The last word snapped out like the crack of a whip. "Teddy, take care of this paper for a minute, will you? Now, Mr. Pettit—"

Muttering under his breath, the lawyer released his hold. Then, as if repenting of his submission, he took a step forward, the blood flooding his face in a crimson wave.

"Just what is the meaning of this behavior?" he exclaimed hotly. "What right have you to break in on us this way? Mr. Looker—"

"Take it slow an' easy, *amigo*," Nick drawled. "They're friends of mine. They got a right to see me any time they want to. Did you want to tell me something, Roy?"

"I sure did!" Roy declared excitedly. "What was this paper you were signing, Nick? Did it have anything to do with your money?"

"Well, yes, it did, Roy." Nick shifted uneasily from one foot to the other. "You see

198

this here waddy offered me fifteen hundred cash if I'd assign my rights to him. He said there wasn't a dog's chance of me ever provin' who I was but that he'd relieve me of the whole thing an' take his chances with the court. He said he'd probably never get anything, but he was willin' to gamble on it. So I thought I'd check out—it's been botherin' me considerable." Nick passed his hand uncertainly through his hair and a frown came to his face. "Wasn't that all right?"

"It was not!" Teddy declared loudly. "He was trying to cheat you, Nick!"

"That's not true!" Pettit shouted, "I wasn't trying to cheat him! He could never prove he's Nicholas Looker. I know the real Nick Looker, but to avoid trouble we were willing to compromise with him. Now he'll not get a cent—not a red cent!"

"So this is the reason you said you were glad my brother and I were out of the way," Roy said slowly, staring hard at the lawyer.

"Eh? What's that? I never said—"

"Oh, yes you did," Teddy interrupted easily. "You and that so-called actor friend of yours. Look at him, Nick, and see if it isn't true!"

Taken by surprise, Pettit lowered his eyes under Nick's gaze and turned away, mumbling.

"See it?" Teddy exclaimed triumphantly. "Thought no one heard you that day down by the station when you and your running-mate were in conference! Well, you're wrong! Here's your hat, Lawyer Pettit, and there's the door!"

"That paper—" Pettit began. But Teddy, with a sudden motion, tore it straight across.

"There's your paper," he said scornfully. "It wasn't signed, anyway. Take it, and get out."

Nick, who stood watching with narrowed eyes, came up to Pettit with clenched fists.

"I got gypped outa' sockin' you before," he murmured. "You came to me with a story of how sorry you were that I misunderstood you when you wanted me to fall for that forgery story, and sayin' that you'd play straight. I believed you—an' by golly you were tryin' to cheat me all the time! Well, here's one chance I won't miss!"

Pettit had been standing with his back to the door. Nick drew back his fist—there was a dull thud, and the lawyer lay on his back on the ground outside the bunkhouse.

"There's a souvenir from me!" Nick cried. "Give him his hat, Teddy—he may catch cold!"

The hat sailed out and landed near the fallen man.

"You—you—" Pettit stuttered, holding his hand to his face. "I'll have the law on you for this! Don't think you can go around assaulting law-abiding people! I'll—"

"You, law-abiding!" Roy said contemptuously. "Why, you're the biggest crook in creation! Try and have the law on us and you'll be up to your neck in hot water! Beat it, you!"

Slowly the lawyer got to his feet. His eyes gleamed evilly. He stood for a moment, looking at the three.

"You hold the cards now," he murmured thickly. "But wait—just wait! That will case comes up in two days, and when it does the only thing you'll get out of it, Nick Looker, will be a smell of dried coffee! Pack that behind the rim of your derby!" And, ramming his hat on his head, Jason Pettit stalked out into the rain.

Teddy, watching him go, bowed low.

"You've got a little surprise waiting for you, Mr. Jason Pettit," he said, grinning. "Nick, we're all set! We've got the proof at last! Listen!"

Nick, with wide eyes, heard the story.

"And I'll get the six thousand after all," he said in a hushed voice when Teddy had finished. "It don't hardly seem possible—it don't hardly! Boys, you sure showed up in the nick of time! Another second an' I'd 'a' had my John Hancock to that paper. Baby! Some close! Now—" he stuck his chin out, and his eyes glittered— "we'll have a little fun with the shyster! In two days, he said—an' all I'd get would be a smell of dried coffee! We'll see about that!

In two days! Boys, let 'em pass quick! I need that money, I do,—at least six hundred of it," he added, in a lower tone.

The days did pass quickly. On Thursday, which was the day following, Tod Jackson and Hank Wall came to the X Bar X. Court opened in Los Dipono on Friday at ten. And on Thursday night Roy and Teddy Manley, Nick Looker, Hank Wall and Tod Jackson started for Los Dipono by auto. They took no chances on being late for court. Hank Wall put them all up in his shop, on cots. Proudly he exhibited the baboon he was stuffing, and Teddy declared it looked as natural as the day he had first seen it in the cabin near Sanborn's Point.

"A lot safer, too," he added. "Break will be pleased to see it," Mr. Wall. When you finish with it you must let us know. Maybe we could buy it and send it to Break for a present!"

On Friday morning the rain stopped and the boys were up and about early. The first person they saw in Los Dipono was Jason Pettit. Roy, coming to the door of Hank's shop, noticed him crossing the street, and called softly to Teddy and Nick. With him was the "actor"—the false Nick Looker. The lawyer's face was swollen, and he glared fiercely at the boys, but did not speak. Roy chuckled.

"Guess he figures he's done enough talking," he said. "Look at that eye! Nick, you sure performed an operation on him! He stared at you as though he'd like to knife you in the back.''

After breakfast all five wandered over to the
court-house. It was only nine o'clock, but Roy
suggested they might as well wait there as any
place. The court-house, if it might be dignified
by such a name, was a two-story structure, with
living rooms on the second floor and the court
on the first. At nine-thirty the janitor opened
the doors, and Roy and the others walked into
court. The room was small, with long benches
as seats for possible spectators. At one side,
in front of two windows, was the judge's desk,
separated from the seats of the common people
by a wooden railing. An American flag was
draped on one of the walls. The place was dark,
dingy, and badly kept, but it was the court of
justice in Los Dipono.

The five companions took places on one of
the benches. Gradually a few more people
drifted in, some with newspapers, some with
worn briefcases. All talked loudly, importantly,
as though matters of great weight were about to
be decided. At a quarter of ten a man, evidently
the clerk of court, entered. Seating himself
on a chair within the railing, he pulled another chair to him to serve as his desk. Then
he extracted a great sheaf of papers from an
inner pocket, planked them down on the floor
beside him, and, leaning carelesly back, he sur-
veyed the people before him with a scornful
eye.

"Maybe that's the judge," Nick whispered. "He looks like a judge."

"Not to me," Teddy laughed. "He's a clerk, or something. Wonder where our friends are?"

"Here they come now," Roy said in a low voice. "Mr. Wall, are those the two you heard talking at the station?"

Hank looked at them carefully.

"Them's them," he pronounced. "Only the tall feller looks different, somehow."

"I did that," Nick chuckled. "Sh! Here comes the judge!"

There was a stir behind them. A short, fat man, with a jovial face, waddled up the aisle. The clerk of court saw him and sprang to his feet.

"Rise, please!" he called pompously. "The court is declared opened!"

CHAPTER XXV

A Jovial Judge's Decision

THE hum of conversation died down as though a heavy blanket had been thrown over the room. The judge adjusted his tie, coughed, and taking a pair of glasses from his pocket, wiped them carefully and put them on.

"What have we to-day, clerk?" he asked, turning to the man at his side. "Give me the things that are ready."

"Well, your honor," the clerk said dubiously, "here are four or five things that have been hanging over. For instance, the case of Clark versus Clark—"

"I thought that was marked no appearance?"

"Oh, yes—so it is—so it is! Hum! Well, your honor—" The clerk moved closer, and lowered his voice so that Teddy and the others could not catch what he said. Then he stepped back, holding in his hand a large envelope.

"In the matter of the will of Julius Looker, deceased!" he called suddenly. "Are the legatees represented here?"

"Teddy, you answer!" Roy whispered quickly.

"Yes, they are!" Teddy exclaimed, jumping to his feet.

"Yes, your honor, they are!" a voice behind Teddy exclaimed. Without turning the boy knew it was Pettit.

The judge looked down over the tops of his glasses.

"Are there contestants?" he asked. "Come forward, young man!" This to Teddy. "Are you a lawyer?"

"No, your honor, I'm not," Teddy answered, feeling his face grow red. Then his courage returned. "But the man named in this will is a friend of mine, and I don't want to see him get cheated out of what belongs to him!"

"Good, good, Teddy!" Roy breathed. "Tell it to him!"

For a moment the judge stared at the boy. Then he smiled.

"That's the spirit," he declared. "Is the beneficiary in court with you?"

"Stand up, Nick!" Roy whispered tensely. But before the cowboy could arise, Pettit was on his feet, talking rapidly.

"Your honor," he was saying, "I wish to protest against this extraordinary proceeding! This boy has no standing in court! I demand that you silence him! The beneficiary of that will is with me. Stand up, Mr. Looker. Here he is, your honor!"

The actor arose and stood staring solemnly

at the judge. By this time the real Nick Looker had also risen, and the court gazed from one to the other in perplexity.

"You each claim you are the Nicholas A. Looker named in this will?" he said slowly.

"That's my name, judge," Nick said shyly. "I was born in Los Dipono. That will was made by my uncle."

"Your honor, again I protest! These people have no standing in court! They should be fined for contempt! I—"

"Now just a minute." The judge raised his hand and gazed at Pettit. "I don't know where you come from, mister, but I reckon it's the East. Maybe you have different methods of procedure there. Maybe they're better—I don't know. But one thing I do know, an' that is that nobody's going to tell me how to run my court! Sit down!"

Pettit's jaw dropped in stunned surprise. He had not expected this. He fell back weakly and pulled his friend to a place beside him.

"Now, son," the judge went on pleasantly to Teddy, "we'll hear your story. Then we'll hear his. It seems that there are two Nicholas A. Lookers. Let's hear your side of it."

"Well, sir," Teddy started eagerly. "Nick Looker, here, is a hand on my father's ranch, near Eagles. His uncle was Julius Looker. Nick was born here, in Los Dipono, although he's been traveling around most of his life, I guess, except these last four years, when he's been with us. We understand that the will leaves six thousand dollars to him, and we'd like to see that he gets it. I guess that's all."

"Teddy, tell him about—" Tod Jackson whispered, but the boy shook his head slightly.

"Later," he answered softly.

Now the judge turned to Pettit.

"What have you got to say to that?"

"It's all false, your honor!" Pettit exclaimed. "This gentleman with me is the real Nicholas Looker. And we can prove it!"

"Prove it, can you?" The judge looked at him interestedly. "How?"

"By this, your honor, his birth certificate!" He passed a paper toward the clerk, who took it and handed it to the judge. Opening it, the judge scanned it quickly.

"This certificate that—hum-twenty-fifth of December-hum-hum-sworn to before me this —hum—well—" He looked up, a queer gleam in his eyes. "It appears regular. Well, son?"

"But it isn't true!" Teddy exclaimed hotly. "Your honor, we have with us a man who has known Nick since he was born—who was present the day he was born—and who can prove this is Nick Looker by a birthmark!"

"You have?" The judge beamed eagerly through his spectacles. "Have him sworn, clerk. I'll hear him."

"But, your honor!" Pettit cried, jumping up. "I protest—"

"Sit down!" the judge thundered. "I'll assess protest fees against you in a minute!" He chuckled, well pleased with his own joke.

As Hank Wall arose, the judge looked at him kindly. He knew of the old taxidermist, of course, as did every one in or near Los Dipono.

"Come right up, Mr. Wall," he said courteously. "No, don't tell me anything until you're sworn," as Hank started to speak.

This function was soon completed, and then, with frequent interruptions by the judge, to bring out more clearly all the details, the story of Nick's birth on that snowy Christmas twenty-seven years ago was told.

"An' he had a black star between his shoulder blades," Hank finished. "I ain't seen it to this day, but I know it's there!"

"On your oath, you've never seen it since?" The judge asked, looking at the old man keenly.

"Not once, Jake!" Hank said earnestly.

A snicker arose from the spectators, which was soon quelled by the clerk calling! "Silence, please!"

The judge thought for a moment. Then pushing back his chair, he arose.

"Mr. Looker, come with me," he said to Nick. "We can soon settle this. Clerk, see that order is kept."

Nick stepped forward eagerly. The judge

opened a side door for him, and the two men passed into a small room. Pettit, his face twitching, leaped to his feet.

"This is an outrage!" he shouted. "I demand—"

The clerk looked at him calmly, and then casually drew from his pocket a heavy pistol and carefully laid it on the chair before him.

"I guess you'd better sort of sit down," he drawled.

Pettit sat down.

In another moment Nick and the judge returned. Nick was grinning widely as he took his seat beside Roy.

"Jinks!" he said in a low voice but excitedly, "I never knew I had that mark on me! But I have! I got it! Right between my shoulder blades! Snakes! Wasn't that—"

"Silence!" the clerk boomed. The judge cleared his throat, adjusted his glasses, and leaned forward.

"Nick Looker—both of you—come forward," he said solemnly. With your representatives."

"That means you, Teddy," Tod Jackson exclaimed. "Go ahead!"

Teddy walked slowly toward the desk, followed by Nick, and took his place on the right. Pettit and his client stepped to the left.

"Gentlemen," the judge said, "I have come to my decision. In me is vested the power of this great, sovereign state to act as an arbitrator

in matters concerning wills. It is the judgment of this court—" he raised his voice—"that
the six thousand dollars is to be given to this
man, as beneficiary under the will of his uncle,
Julius Looker!" He pointed directly at Nick.

"Good fer you, Jake!" Hank Wall piped
shrilly. "Good fer—"

"Silence!"

"And it is the further judgment of this
court," the judge continued, turning now to
Pettit, "that this man be fined one hundred
dollars for contempt, with the option of standing trial for forgery! At the date of this birth
certificate we had no such record in Los
Dipono!"

"But—but—" Pettit stuttered. Then he saw
how he had been caught. Words were useless.
"I'll pay," he muttered. "But it was all this
fool's fault." He pointed to the man at his
side. "He wanted me to do it. I'd have
never—"

"Would you rather pay two hundred?" the
judge asked sweetly. "No? Then apply that
old adage—silence is golden!"

The actor, his face white, glanced at his
lawyer.

"Fool, am I?" he said in a low voice. "Come
outside! You know this was all your plan—
that you told me in New York about some easy
money we would pick up here. Then you pull
a bonehead play like that—a birth certificate

when they didn't have such things! You ninny!
I got a good mind to—''

"Ninny, is it!" Pettit shouted. "It's not
enough that you get me fined one hundred dollars, but you also call me—''

"Clerk, take 'em out!" the judge snapped.

The clerk arose lazily, and then, for the first
time, the boys noticed how large he was. Carelessly he seized a collar of each of the arguing
men. Suddenly he stiffened. There was a
wild flinging about of legs and arms, and Pettit
and his friend went sailing out of the room,
victims of the old-fashioned, but ever popular,
"bum's rush"!

This time there was no one to cry "silence!"
and the whole court, not excepting the judge,
rocked with laughter. Pettit and his client had
disappeared into the great unknown. The last
glimpse the boys had of them was of their flying
coat tails.

When order had once more been restored the
judge descended from the bench and shook
Teddy's hand.

"My boy," he said earnestly, "I want to
compliment you. It is due to you that Mr.
Looker is the richer by six thousand dollars.
You deserve his sincere thanks."

"My brother helped as much as I did!"
Teddy said quickly. "But actually, I guess
Hank Wall was the cause of the whole thing.
He's the hero of the day."

The old man heard, and stood up proudly. He nodded his white head and glanced about him. His eyes twinkled.

"This is the second time I been in court," he declared. "I'm gettin' to like it. It's too bad there wasn't a lawyer to ask me questions —could 'a' fooled him proper. I'm clever at legal questions—mighty clever. By jinks, I got an idea! Jake, you know what I'm goin' to be?"

"What?" the judge asked, an amused smile on his face. Hank Wall hesitated a moment, saw that every one in the court room was listening, put his hand to his white beard and said, with a chuckle:

"A lawyer, that's what! Yes sir, a lawyer— when I grow up!"

Into the yard of the X Bar X four persons drove. They were talking loudly, happily. Teddy and Roy were in front, with Tod Jackson and Nick Looker in the rear of the auto. Hank Wall had, of course, been left at his home in Los Dipono after Tod had paid him for his part in the pictures and with instructions to finish stuffing the ape, which Tod declared he wished to purchase. When Teddy suggested it would make a unique wedding present, the actor blushed and declared:

"Bessie would refuse to live with me if I gave her that. I want to get it for Break. If he ever slows up in his work as a comedian, he can look at that, and remember!''

So intent were the four on their own affairs that they were unaware of three men who, mounted, sat watching them from a distant hill. One of the trio, biting a generous chunk from a plug of tobacco, turned to his companion.

''Where they been, Denver?'' he asked.

In a high-pitched voice came the answer, the speaker's face twisted in a sneer:

''Court! I followed 'em to Los Dipono an' saw 'em go in. Poor fishes! After us, most likely! What a chance—what a chance! They don't even know we're here! Come on! Gonna hang around here all day? We'll get 'em later —an' get 'em good! Mosey, now!''

Three horses swung around. Another moment and the riders were out of sight. Whether Denver Smith made good his threat or not will be told in the next volume of this series, to be called ''The X Bar X Boys at the Round-Up.''

Later that day Teddy, Roy, Belle, Ethel and Nell were walking toward the bunkhouse. Tod Jackson had said farewell and had promised to visit the boys if he ever came West again. He carried with him their best wishes for the success of the moving picture company—especially of Break O'Day.

''Tell him to keep that Adam's apple of his in good shape!'' Roy had called, laughing. And

Tod, riding off, said he would. The boys were sorry to see him go. He had been a real friend —a "regular fellow," as Teddy put it.

As Belle and the others neared the bunkhouse Roy asked:

"Wonder what Nick is going to do with that money? I know he gave some of it to Jules Kolto, so he could pay his debt to dad, but I saw him talking to dad a little later, and he had a wad of bills in his hand. There's no place to spend it around here. Maybe—"

"Listen!" Belle interrupted, holding up her finger. "Isn't that Nick's voice?"

Within the shack an excited conversation was taking place. Teddy and Roy stepped nearer, and looked in.

Pop Burns stood over a bench, three cards in his hands. About him were grouped Bug Eye, Nat Raymond, Sing Lung, the cook; Gus Tripp, Jules Kolto, Jim Casey, and—Nick. In Nick's hand was a sheaf of greenbacks.

"Now, boys," Pop monotoned, "I ain't hypnotized this time. I think you are. Anyway, you can't tell me where the ace of spades falls. Watch 'em—watch 'em close! Blooey! Which one?"

"The middle!" Nick shouted, planking down a bill. "Ten bucks on the middle card!"

The boys turned away, grinning.

"You were wondering what Nick would do with his money. He'll find a use for it," Teddy chuckled. "See what he's doing, Roy? He knows the boys wouldn't take it from him as a gift, so he's losing it to them! Good old Nick! That's friendship, by golly! Whatever Pop wins he'll split with the others. In that way Nick'll share his good fortune. The good old sport! Oh, boy, there's the supper bell! I'm some hungry. Come on, let's go!"

They walked toward the ranch house. Belle, Ethel and Nell entered first, and Teddy and Roy stood on the porch for a moment. Teddy grinned as a loud, determined voice reached their ears.

"I got it! I got it now! Here we are, Pop! Sure this time! Luck, stay with me! Ten bucks on the middle card!"

Nick was dividing his money, or at least a good share of it. But safely tucked away in his shirt he had six hundred dollars awaiting the return of Ham Kidder.

THE END

WESTERN STORIES FOR BOYS

By JAMES CODY FERRIS

Each Volume Complete in Itself.

Thrilling tales of the great west, told primarily for boys but which will be read by all who love mystery, rapid action, and adventures in the great open spaces.

The cowboys of the X Bar X Ranch are real cowboys, on the job when required, but full of fun and daring—a bunch any reader will be delighted to know.

THE X BAR X BOYS ON THE RANCH
THE X BAR X BOYS IN THUNDER CANYON
THE X BAR X BOYS ON WHIRLPOOL RIVER
THE X BAR X BOYS ON BIG BISON TRAIL
THE X BAR X BOYS AT THE ROUND-UP
THE X BAR X BOYS AT NUGGET CAMP
THE X BAR X BOYS AT RUSTLER'S GAP
THE X BAR X BOYS AT GRIZZLY PASS
THE X BAR X BOYS LOST IN THE ROCKIES
THE X BAR X BOYS RIDING FOR LIFE
THE X BAR X BOYS IN SMOKY VALLEY
THE X BAR X BOYS AT COPPERHEAD GULCH
THE X BAR X BOYS BRANDING THE WILD HERD
THE X BAR X BOYS AT THE STRANGE RODEO
THE X BAR X BOYS WITH THE SECRET RANGERS
THE X BAR X BOYS HUNTING THE PRIZE
    MUSTANGS

GROSSET & DUNLAP   *Publishers*   NEW YORK

On the Trail of Clues and Criminals

Illustrated. Every Volume Complete in Itself.

Frank and Joe Hardy are sons of a celebrated detective. Often the boys help him in his investigations. In their spare hours and during vacations they follow up clues "on their own hook." These activities lead them into many strange adventures and dangerous situations. Yet their efforts are usually successful in tracking down criminals. These stories are packed with action, adventure and mystery.

THE HARDY BOYS STORIES

By FRANKLIN W. DIXON

THE TOWER TREASURE
THE HOUSE ON THE CLIFF
THE SECRET OF THE OLD MILL
THE MISSING CHUMS
HUNTING FOR HIDDEN GOLD
THE SHORE ROAD MYSTERY
THE SECRET OF THE CAVES
THE MYSTERY OF CABIN ISLAND
THE GREAT AIRPORT MYSTERY
WHAT HAPPENED AT MIDNIGHT
WHILE THE CLOCK TICKED
FOOTPRINTS UNDER THE WINDOW
THE MARK ON THE DOOR
THE HIDDEN HARBOR MYSTERY
A FIGURE IN HIDING

GROSSET & DUNLAP   *Publishers*   NEW YORK

TALES OF ADVENTURE IN THE GREAT NORTHWEST
By JAMES OLIVER CURWOOD

THE GRIZZLY KING
The story of Thor, the biggest grizzly in the Rockies, and the hunter who pursued but never shot him.

NOMADS OF THE NORTH
Neewa, the bear cub, and Miki, the pup, separated from their master, grow up in the wilderness until, in the end, they find him and bring to him the girl he loves.

SWIFT LIGHTNING
The adventures of a wolf in whose veins is a drop of dog blood. His desperate combats and killings, and his mating with a lost collie make a tale of breathless suspense.

THE WOLF HUNTERS
A tenderfoot, a young Indian and their faithful guide battle courageously with a savage band of outlaw Indians in the Canadian wilderness.

THE GOLD HUNTERS
A search for a lost gold mine leads the three heroes of "The Wolf Hunters" on a hazardous trail of mystery and amazing adventure.

BACK TO GOD'S COUNTRY
The courage and devotion of Wapi, the wolf dog, saves the life of a woman imprisoned on an ice-bound ship in the Far North.

THE GOLDEN SNARE
Philip Raine, of the Royal Northwest Mounted Police, taken prisoner by the murderer he is pursuing, finds strange adventure with a half-mad wolf-man, a beautiful girl and a courageous Swede.

GROSSET & DUNLAP   *Publishers*   NEW YORK

FOOTBALL AT ITS BEST
"Hot Off The Gridiron" Stories

UNDER THE GOAL POSTS
by EDDIE DOOLEY
A rousing story of college football by a great player.

By HAROLD M. SHERMAN
ONE MINUTE TO PLAY
There wasn't room in Red Wade's trunk for his football togs and his textbooks too—so he left his textbooks at home!

TOUCHDOWN!
A thrilling, smashing, breath-taking football story—introducing the "big three."

BLOCK THAT KICK!
Tingling romance, breath-taking mystery. Climaxed by a championship football game at the Yankee Stadium.

CRASHING THROUGH!
How a clever little quarterback kept his big rivals' fighting spirit at high pitch in order that his eleven might win a big game.

FIGHT 'EM, BIG THREE
Plenty of action on the gridiron and in other fields also. A story of three youths, Stuffy, Pepper and Brick.

GOAL TO GO!
Shrimp and Tubby, the "David and Goliath" of the Merwin College eleven, bring a great football crowd to its feet shouting like mad.

HOLD THAT LINE!
A story of the heart-breaking and nerve-trying experience one college player underwent before success.

NUMBER 44
How Bun Ritter, former mascot, becomes as famous as the mighty Branson, makes a story packed with football sensation!

GROSSET & DUNLAP   *Publishers*   NEW YORK